For those who believe in me, you're

the reason I'm alive.

Chapter 1

It was chaos. The restaurant was filled with Redskin fans. Red everywhere. Hats, jerseys, the booths, even the plastic cups. This place was loud. Cheers and hollers came from the mouth of college kids and grown men having one too many beers.

There I was in the booth with my dad. He didn't have on red anything. We were traveling from Washington D.C. back home to Middletown, Connecticut. The only reason we are this far from home is that Daddy told me we had to hide from the bad guys for a little while. Daddy said he owed them some money, but payday hasn't come around yet, so we had to hide out until then.

All of my stuff was in the car. My blanket, pillow, some of my winter clothes because it was cold in D.C. We were sleeping in Daddy's car. He told me I had to pack heavier clothes, so I would stay warm at night time. Daddy would sing songs on the radio while his fingers tapped the steering wheel. I would brush Katy, who was my kitty stuffed animal, I named her after me. Daddy always called me Kat, so I thought it would be fun to name my cat that, too. I would brush her while listening to the pitch of Daddy's voice go up and down. I brought Kat inside the restaurant with me. Daddy smiles when I bring her places.

He took me to see the White House and a big tall building with a big pool in front of it. It was cold out there, but Daddy took pictures of me and Kat standing in front of these places so it's something I can always keep in my treasure box. Mommy will be excited to see them. I miss Mommy.

I was much younger than all of the boys here at the restaurant. These boys don't pay much attention to a little girl who's only seven and three quarters. That was ok, Daddy talked to me. He would ask me if I was okay and if I liked my fries.

The fries were much better than the last place we ate. It's a good thing Daddy didn't have to pay for them. He told the waitress he was taking me to the potty and we didn't go back to the table. Daddy said we didn't have to pay for the fries because they were so bad. Daddy always knew how to save money. There's sometimes when we get gas he tells me that gas is bad, and we don't have to pay for that either. He's smart.

This place had good fries though. I drank my milkshake and dipped my fries in ketchup. The ketchup was red, too! I really like this place. I like red. It reminds me of the red car where me and my daddy used to sleep before we got this new car.

The new car is nicer. It's gold. I like gold. The gold car doesn't have plastic on the windows so it's much quieter when the rain hits the windows than when it was hitting the plastic bags. There's a much bigger back seat, too. I sleep better back there.

"Kat, I need to go talk to that man right over there. I'll be right back. Will you be okay for a few minutes?" Daddy asked. I shook my head yes while I tried to blow bubbles in my milkshake. It wasn't working out too well for me.

Daddy got up and headed over to the counter. The counter is shaped like a U. There are booths on both sides of the counters looking outside. There are big tall tables sitting in front of the counters. We were sitting on the right side by the back door. It was chilly every time someone opened the door, so I kept my coat on.

Daddy talked to a man in a red and white hat. He wasn't very tall. He had a book in his hand with a little pencil. I've seen pencils like that before at the mini-golf place we went to one time. I want a small pencil like that. I wonder if the red hat man has an extra?

The man started writing something down in his book with his little pencil and I saw Daddy give him some money. Maybe Daddy knew I wanted that pencil and he bought it for me! But Daddy came back over with no pencil. It was okay though, I had these crayons to do my word search with on this placemat.

Daddy said we were going to be here for a little while. I didn't mind. It was warm in here and these booths were bouncy. My feet couldn't touch the floor just yet, so I just let them swing. Our booth was next to a window and I could see outside. There were many cars driving up and down the interstate. I bet they were going to their homes, too. The parking lot was full of cars from everyone in the restaurant. There was a gas station across the street where big trucks would pull in and out. I liked to watch them turn their tires.

There was a woman outside in the parking lot. She was in a blue car with no top. She must be cold. It's really windy here and I thought I was going to blow away walking inside. Luckily, Daddy held my hand. Her daddy wasn't there to hold her hand. Her shoulder length, gold, curly hair was blowing all over her face.

She saw me. She smiled and waved to me through the glass. She was missing a tooth. Daddy was missing a tooth. I hope she didn't lose her tooth by getting hit in the mouth like Daddy did. Daddy was in pain for a while. I had to get him a bag of frozen corn to put on his lip to make him feel better. I take care of Daddy like Daddy takes care of me.

She looked sad. She was standing by her car with the hood up. I bet one of these men in here could help her fix her car. They were watching the game right now, but I bet afterward they could help her out.

The buzzer sounded on the t.v. and it scared me. Daddy yelled at the t.v. and then looked at me and giggled. He saw the lady outside, too. He looked sad when he saw her. I should tell him she can sleep with us in the car if she can't get home. Daddy might get mad though. Daddy doesn't really let girls come around since Mommy left.

Mommy got mad at Daddy one day. I remember them yelling and Mommy was crying. She came and kissed me and told me she would see me soon. I miss Mommy, but she'll be back soon. Daddy said she's got some things to do and will be back when she's done. That's okay sometimes I have to do things like clean my room before I can come back out and play with Daddy.

The waitress came over and asked if I wanted some water. I shook my head yes, again. I didn't like to talk much to strangers. Daddy always told me that people are only worried about themselves and that I need to worry about myself. But, I worry about Daddy. He doesn't sleep much and he's always checking his wallet. I asked him one time if he was keeping a fairy in there. He told me I was a silly girl. I smiled when he called me Silly. Daddy always knew how to make me smile.

The woman outside started to walk in the door behind me. She walked over to the counter and asked if she could use the phone. Her voice was funny. It sounded like my lunch lady at school. She sounded like an elephant my friend Steph would say. It was loud and trunky. But she meant to say husky is what Daddy said.

I heard her on the phone. She was upset. She told whoever on the phone her name was Carol. That was easy to remember. Carol with the curls. She slammed the phone back on the hook and sat down on one of the stools at the counter. She looked over this way. Daddy nodded to her and tipped his hat. Daddy had on a blue hat with a C on it. I told him it needs to have a K on it for Kat. Carol smiled back.

I went back to my word search and the game came back on the t.v. Daddy would cheer and then groan. He would cheer again and then groan, again. The buzzer only got louder.

Curly Carol was still sitting at the counter. She still looked mad but every once in a while, she would look over at me and smile again. I like her.

I looked at words in my word search. All of the words had to do with the Redskins. Football, quarterback, receiver, I didn't know what they meant but Daddy seemed to know. Daddy started getting upset and banging his hand on the table. I had to potty. I didn't want to bother him. I looked around for the bathroom. It was behind me by the back door. I bet I could sneak off and Daddy wouldn't notice.

Curly Carol must have seen me looking around because she walked over to our table. "Do you need to potty, sweetheart? I'm headed that way right now if you want to come with me." She looked at Daddy.

"Yeah, yeah, that's fine. Go ahead Kat," he said while weaving his head back and forth around Carol trying to see the tv.

Curly Carol reached her hand out for me to hold. It was soft and warm. She seemed really nice.

"My name is Carol. What's yours?" she asked.

"Katy. But Daddy calls me Kat." I said while walking into the bathroom.

"Well, Kat. It's nice to meet you. Do you need help in there or will you be okay?"

"I'll be ok." I walked into the stall and did my business. I came out and washed my hands. Carol walked out of her stall and washed her hands, too. The air dryer was warm on my hands. I really liked being warm. Carol must have noticed my smile.

"Are you cold, Kat?"

"I'm always cold Miss Carol. My blanket in the car has a hole in it so I get cold sometimes. I usually wear my coat when I'm sleeping." I said.

"Where do you sleep?" she looked confused. I told her about how we were sleeping in the car until we could get back home to Connecticut. She said she had an extra blanket out in the car and asked if I wanted it. I told her that would be nice, but she might need it in case she needs to sleep in her car. "Now, Katy, I can always go get me another blanket. Why don't you just take the one I have?"

"Daddy says we don't need to take things from other people. That I need to worry about myself and that others need to worry about themselves. You should worry that if you get cold you have a blanket in your car." I said.

She grabbed me and hugged me. Her body was warm, too. I really liked Curly Carol. She walks me back to my table and told me that if I needed to potty again just to ask her and that she would be sitting right there at the counter if I needed her.

Daddy was really upset. I looked up at the t.v. and saw the Redskins were losing by 2. That must be why he is upset. There wasn't very much longer in the game. Daddy told me it was his turn to potty. He got out of the booth, leaned over and kissed my head. "I love you, Kat."

"I love you, too, Daddy," I said. Daddy walked back to the bathroom. I felt the cold air come through the door and I shivered a bit. I heard a loud car outside. I thought it was the trucks across the street, but it looked like Daddy's gold car leaving. But, it couldn't be Daddy because he was in the bathroom.

I sat there for a little bit and the crowd started to growl a bit more. Curly Carol kept turning around to check on me. I would just smile at her and she would smile back. I bet she would like the little Kat as well. I pretend to feed little Kat some french fries and would get back to work searching for words.

Some of the people were starting to head out the door now that the game was almost over. I figured we would be leaving soon to when Daddy got out of the bathroom, so I got my things together. Sometimes Daddy likes to leave really fast, so I've learned to be ready to go.

It started to get really quiet in the restaurant and then suddenly, "BUUUUUZZZZZZZZ."

I sat up from my sleep and looked around anxiously. My alarm was going off. I looked at the time and I was going to be late.

Chapter 2

I was running across campus in hopes I wouldn't be late. I had my leg warmers on and my sweater over my leotard. I had to be ready to jump on the stage as soon as I walked in the auditorium.

I had just gotten the lead role in the schools' drama, 'Dancer in the Night'. It was about a girl who had a desire to be a dancer and run a performance at the Infinity Hall in Hartford, Connecticut. Not that my alter ego would be opposed to dancing like a stripper, but this was a little more classy. I run up the stairs of the Ice Auditorium and sling open the door. Immediately to my right is a U-shaped staircase going down and I take two steps at a time. I open up the basement door and take an immediate left into the dressing room.

I open the door and there sits Rey. She is my best friend in the play, in real life, and my roommate. "Why didn't you wake me up?!" I yelled.

"I tried! You kept whimpering in your sleep. I figured you were having another dream, so I left you alone. Relax. Toby came in and said Director Mark wasn't even here yet. I guess last night's storm blew out his power. So, you have time to do your makeup." she responded.

I let out a sigh of relief and walked over to my vanity chair. The dressing room was made up of two vanities. One on the left side, one on the right with just enough room for two people to stand in between them to do hair. At the end of the walkway was a clothing rack where we kept our wardrobes. I sat my stuff down next to the vanity on the left.

My vanity was cream with lights around the mirror. My makeup brushes sat neatly in their holders and my hot irons were kept in the cup off to the side of the vanity. My makeup was kept in a trunk right in front of the mirror for easy access.

"When is Mark supposed to be here?" I didn't call him 'Director' like Rey. Mark was more of a friend to me than an acquaintance. He was one of the first people I met in my drama classes before he graduated and became a director here at Midtown University. He and I are the same age, but I didn't start college until he was graduating college. I wanted to experience life for a bit. However, that basically meant me switching between painting and dancing on the roof of my mom's apartment building. It's weird that this play is exactly my dreams, but then again Mark knew this, so is it really a coincidence?

"Toby said it would be closer to 9," Rey responded. Rey was a pretty girl. She had the stereotypical body type of a dancer. Long legs, thin frame, sharp jawline with beautiful long blonde, icy strands on her flawless face. She makes me mad just looking at her. While here I am short with dark curly hair. Sometimes I don't even know if I have a jawline. I'm pretty sure I have a gobbler face like a turkey.

"I must have fallen asleep pretty early last night. I think the storm made me comfortable." I said. Storms have always been my thing even back when I was a girl. I could sleep through any storm while riding in the car. Something about the rain hitting the window calms me. "I didn't even finish writing my literature paper that's due at midnight tonight."

"Well, you better do something about it quick, because Toby's birthday is today, and we already made reservations at Pollo Vallarta and you are going," Rey reminded me.

"Shit." I tried to plan in my head when and how I was going to manage to get everything done knowing that rehearsal was going to last until at least lunch. "What time is dinner? I don't even have anything to wear. I still have laundry to do."

"Will you chill? Dinner is at seven o'clock. You have plenty of time. Take your laptop to the laundry mat and write your paper while you wait. Just shower when you get back to the apartment." Rey had it all figured out. Thank goodness she is my roommate and best friend. She's more like a sister. I've known her since I was eight years old. She was nice to me when I switched schools and became friends when we were in the same dance class as a child.

A knock on the door and Toby stuck in his head. "Guys, Director is here. We're ready." Toby is a set construction manager for the play. He and Mark met during undergrad and have worked many dramas since. Toby is a short, beefy guy. He has dark hair and a clean-shaven face. I like Toby. His boyfriend, Cori, is my love interest in the play.

I head towards the stage to start rehearsal. Mark meets me at the curtain. He's standing there right at six feet tall with short dark hair with a short scruffy goatee. "Katy," he says with his stern deep voice.

"Mark," I respond staring deep into his brown eyes. I've always been attracted to him. We have flirted on and off throughout the years, but he was dating someone until recently. I think he might be into me a little bit, but I'm not interested in dating anyone. Especially in this environment. It's weird enough having to kiss people you hardly know on stage in front of people but to do it in front of your significant other could put a strain on your relationship. Not to mention you're trying to trust someone in a new relationship, and chemistry on stage could lead to false indications of cheating or mixed feelings.

"Will you be joining us tonight to celebrate Toby's day of birth?" he asked.

"That's if I can get my literature paper done in time. And laundry. And shower. But right now, my main goal is to get this over with, so I can eat lunch." I winked and walked through the curtain.

Mark followed through and jumped off stage to sit in the third row. "Hit the music!"

I hurried home after grabbing a sub at the local deli. Our apartment is located downtown above the deli. There is an entrance out front and it leads upstairs to an apartment. I run upstairs and grabbed my laundry along with my laptop and head down the street to Wash N Roll. I really needed to concentrate on my paper, but it was chaos at the laundromat. I short-sentenced my notes, submitted my paper and closed the notebook. I looked at my phone to see the time. It was already after four. I still have time to shower.

Our apartment has only one bathroom. It's a simple place. We are the only apartment through the entrance from the street. The living room has white walls with a white shag rug over the gray carpet with a four-legged, wood apothecary coffee table. Our couch is white, but we've added a pop of color with the bohemian throw pillows.

There are bookshelves across from the couch, instead of a television, in the living room. The building attached to ours is a bookstore. We are constantly on the watch for the table of ninety-nine cent clearance books.

The walls have dream catchers and paintings of birds. The living room leads right into the kitchen. White walls, with white cabinets and appliances. The cabinets wrap around to make a bar with two barstools connecting to the living room. There's not enough room for a kitchen table. To the left is the hallway. My bedroom is on the left overlooking the street and Rey's is across from mine overlooking the alley. Her room is bigger, but I preferred the street view. Our bathroom is at the end of the hallway between our two rooms.

I believe a person's space should reflect their personality. If you're modern, you should have modern decor, if you are classy, stick with pearls and crystals, if you have a dark soul, surround yourself with warm colors. The living room, kitchen, and bathroom have all been remodeled, but the bedrooms still have brick outer walls. I love the older, vintage décor.

I found an antique vanity on the side of the road. I called Rey and we carried it seven blocks back to the apartment. It's a cherry walnut color with a large oval mirror. I bought a piece of multi-colored fabric and stapled it to the chair I found with it. I wiped it down with pine-sol and voila; it's probably my favorite piece in the apartment. My bed has a gray metal headboard leaned up against the wall. My sheets and comforter are bright oranges with pops of blue. My throw pillows are mixture of burgundy and yellow. My chest is turquoise and has orange candlesticks I found at a yard sale and spray painted. As weary as the weather is here in Middletown, I like to have something that reminds me of the sun all year 'round.

I open up my closet that sits to the right of my headboard. My closet's size can only be compared to the size of my armpit. Luckily, I have a limited amount of clothes that I actually wear on a daily basis. Naturally, I have nothing to wear tonight. My wardrobe consists of dance flats, leggings, and sweaters. I have one pair of boots and a pair of Crocs. It's really time that I go shopping. That would be nice if I had a job.

I'm currently living off student loans because I thought it would be a great idea to quit my job and dedicate myself to this play. I worked at the movie theater in town. I had worked there since I was in high school. As much as I despised the hours, the people, the smell of popcorn embedded into the threads of my clothes, it was stable and easy.

I pulled a pair of yellow jeggings and a simple brown cami from my chester drawers. I opened my closet and found a maroon cardigan. This may not be classified as a spring wardrobe but it's just about the most sophisticated outfit I have, unless my last year's Easter dress I found at the thrift store, is appropriate for a fiesta.

I take my time getting ready for tonight's festivities. I flat ironed my short curly brown hair only to re-curl with beach waves. I decided to be daring tonight and wear mascara. My typical made-up face it's usually a pressed powder and bronzer. I have my eyeliner tattooed on, so I normally don't wear mascara. I feel frisky tonight. I throw on my pair of tan knee-high boots and grab my crossbody purse and head out the door.

Rey had a late afternoon class, so she packed a bag and got ready in the auditorium dressing room. She plans on meeting me there. I lock the front door and head down the stairs. I head towards the restaurant which is about four blocks away.

I have a car, but I rarely use it. It's my mom's old two-door Ford Escort. I'm pretty sure it was made the year I was born but I've always been too scared to ask. I'm thankful she gave it to me, but if I have the opportunity to walk, I choose to.

Middletown is a timely town. Brick buildings cover the downtown main streets. Besides the Midtown University on one end of town that is filled with locals, which I attend, and the private university, Rivot, it's a quiet town. R.U. consists of nothing but rich, entitled young adults looking to be the successors of our country.

I've met a few of the students that attend Rivot from working at the theater, but never good enough to care to make conversation with any of them. I'm not into the sweaters around the neck with khaki and suede shoes. I'm more into the jeans, t-shirt, and ballcap like Mark wears.

Ah, Mark, I'm actually looking forward to seeing him outside of the theater. It'll be nice to communicate about other things than him yelling at me for not standing on my mark. It's been so long since he hasn't used a high pitch voice at me, it might actually be weird to hear him talk in normal tone for an extended period of time.

I notice there's a help wanted sign in the window of the book store. I will stop in there tomorrow and apply. The hours couldn't be as bad as the movie theater so it's worth a shot.

Daylight starts to fade, and the wind starts to pick up as I get closer to the restaurant. I walk in the doors to see Rey, Toby, Cori, Mark, and Carson. Carson is one of Mark's friends. He works on the set with Toby and Mark. I'm pretty sure Rey has a crush on him but she's too stubborn to tell me if she does.

"There she is," Rey address. "We just ordered a couple pitchers of margaritas, grab a seat."

I sit down next to Rey across from Mark. A part of my stomach flutters. Why am I being such a school girl? I've known him, for what seems like, forever. Maybe I'm just lonely. I haven't had a boyfriend since freshman year. I wouldn't technically call him a boyfriend. He was basically a convenient hook up that would buy me pizza on the Tuesday nights we saw each other.

"Katy." Mark looked at me with his devilish blue eyes.

"Mark."

The waitress brought our pitchers over to the table. Laughs start to get louder as the pitchers seem to empty. Toby had his picture taken in his sombrero and ate his free fried ice cream. The margaritas went down smoothly but I switched to beer after the first pitcher was gone. Mark and I tease each other back and forth as Rey nonchalantly winks at me in the process. Rey and Carson are flirting heavily as well as me and Mark. I smile when looking at him and he grins with an ornery look in his eyes. This has been fun. Maybe too much fun. I stand up to pay my bill and I wasn't prepared to be drunk.

"Whoa," I laugh. "Mark, can you be of assistance, please?" Mark laughs and stands only to find himself wobbling, as well. I laugh at him while he tries to act manly and coherent. He wraps his arm around my waist and walks to me the counter. I reach for my wallet, but Mark stops me.

"I've got it, " he demands.

"No, no, that's not necessary. I can pay for my food and drinks. I'm a big girl."

"Don't argue," he says as he takes my bill out of my hand and pays the girl behind the counter.

"Fine. But, I owe you drinks, or food, or drinks, or food."

"You *are* drunk!" he exclaims.

"Noooo, you *are* drunk. I'm just fine," I say touching his nose.

I wobble back to the table and tell everyone goodbye. Mark offers to walk me home, but I was adamant about him not coming back with me. As lonely as I was, I wasn't doing anything out of loneliness. It would just make Monday's rehearsal awkward. Rey and Carson decide they are going to continue the party at the bar across the street from Pollo Vallarta.

It had rained during the time we were eating. So, not only am I wobbling, I'm not weeble wobbling around puddles. I make it through the first two blocks just fine. I have to stop and take a breather next to the mail receptacle. I must look suspicious because a cop car pulls up next to me. He turns off the car and approaches me.

"Are you ok, ma'am?" the officer said.

I stop in my tracks.

He was the sexiest man I have ever seen.

Chapter 3

"Ma'am?" the officer questions as he steps in front of me.

I feel it coming on. There's no stopping it. Here I go. There's no time to tell him to move. I vomit all over his shoes.

I try to regain my balance as he has grabs my arm to keep me standing up. The intensity runs right through me but I'm too inebriated to understand anything but vomiting. The only thing I feel right now is my head spinning.

"Is this a joke? Am I being pranked right now," he says annoyed. "No? No one out there messing with me? Unbelievable." Yep, he's definitely aggravated. Ok, let's get you home." he states. "Do you have a name?"

"Katy. Do *you* have a name?"

"Officer Lakes," he says. "Well, Katy, I really don't appreciate you ruining my shoes. I should give you a citation for public intoxication, but I feel like you wouldn't remember it anyways." He's trying to keep his composure and not laugh. "I'm not going to take you to jail, you'd probably just puke in my car. Do you know where you live?"

I look up to see where I am. I see the book store on my block. "I live right there. I can get there. Watch me. " I pause and look at his face. Oh, he's handsome. He's got eyes and hair and a nose that I could kiss. I think they're all dark. I think everything is dark. It is dark outside. Lights. We need lights. He should know this. "Lights! We need lights! Turn on your lights. It's dark everywhere."

"That's because your eyes are closed."

"HA! I'm funny," as I stumble a few more feet.

"Do you have your keys?" he asks as we get to my outside street door.

"Do you have *your* keys?" I chuckle. I fumble through my purse and find my keys.

"Let's get you upstairs." He takes the keys and unlocks the outside door. "Do you have any dogs I need to worry about?" he asks as we walk up the stairs.

"No. I have a stuffed cat."

"Well, I think I can handle that." He unlocks the interior door and we walk inside. "Ok, you're home now. Are you going to be ok? Do you need a trash can? We don't want you ruining your rug like you did my shoes."

"You've got jokes, Officer Lakes. I don't need a trash-" I feel it rising up my throat again. I make a break for it down the hall to the bathroom. I make it in time to lift the lid and it spews from my mouth. It takes like queso dip and tequila. I hope Officer Lovely doesn't walk in here.

"Katy?" I hear him getting closer. "Katy, I got you some water. Is there someone I can call for you?"

I flush the toilet and grab onto the sink to pull myself up. I turn on the cold water and splash some on my face. I wipe my mouth on the hand towel and throw it in the floor. I remember his shoes and wet a washcloth for him. I ring it out and open the door. Officer Lakes is standing against the wall with a glass of ice water in his hand. He's young. He can't be older than 25 or 26. He has his hat sitting on top of his head as if he's recently scratched his forehead. His short dark hair is exposed. He turns to look at me. His blue eyes are piercing. His facial hair is trimmed sharp around his jawline. I'm suddenly sober.

"Sorry about your shoes." I hand him the washcloth in exchange for the glass of water in his hand. "I'm okay. Thank you. Rey will be home soon." I turn to the right and flip on my light. I lean up against my dresser and start to take off my shoes.

"Is Rey your boyfriend?" he asks, and he kneels to wipe off his shoes.

"You're funny. Rey is my *female* roommate. She lives there." I point across the hall. "I live here," pointing to my bed.

"Alright, Miss-I never got your last name?" he points out as he stands up and tosses the puke-covered washcloth onto the bathroom floor.

"Cambridge. Katy Cambridge." I flip my shoes off, set my cell phone on my nightstand, fluff my pillow and pull my blankets back.

"Well, Miss Cambridge, I hope you feel better. And let's try not to puke anymore."

I crawl into bed, fully dressed "will you please lock the door on the way out, Officer--Lakes? Am I right?"

"Yes, Chad Lakes. I will lock the door on my way out. Goodnight Katy." He flips off the light and heads back towards the living room.

I yell "Goodnight Chad!" I hear the living room door close.

I wake up with a killer headache. I roll over to check my phone. I never plugged it in last night. Ugh, it's nine fifteen. It's not even close to the time I want to be awake. It's Saturday so that means no rehearsal today. The only thing I have planned for today is running downstairs to the bookstore to apply for the vacant position. I try to recall last night's happenings. Then suddenly my eyes open wide.

Captain Lovely. I don't remember what he told me is his real name. I just remember him being gorgeous. And his shoes! How humiliating. I covered him in my vomit. I. Can't. Even. I pull the blankets back over my head and fall back to sleep.

Twelve thirty rolls around and I hear movement in the kitchen. Rey must be up and moving. I don't remember hearing her come in last night. I throw the covers off of me and notice I'm still wearing last night's attire. I open my bedroom door and head towards the kitchen. I hear a male's voice.

"Hey sleepyhead!" Rey is loud. Why didn't I pick a quieter roommate? I see Carson sitting on a barstool while Rey is frying eggs on the stove. "Do you want some eggs?"

I shake my head no and head to the fridge for a bottle of water.

"What happened to you last night? The bar was dead, so we came straight back home. When we were walking back to the apartment we saw a police officer leaving our building. What happened, are you ok?"

I explained to them that Officer Lovely made sure I made it upstairs safely. I told her how I puked on his shoes. She didn't really seem too surprised about that one. I do have a history of vomiting while I'm drunk.

"Carson. Why are you here?" I asked to change the subject from me. "Did you guys finally hook up?"

"Eggs are done, Carson." Rey interrupted. "I put green food coloring in them in honor of St. Patty's Day."

Shit. St. Patrick's Day. She's going to make me drink again tonight. Before she can even say it, I'm going to cut--

"We are going to McVey's Pub," tonight. Do you have anything green to wear?" Damn it, Rey.

"I'm never drinking, again.... Again."

"Horseshit. Drink some water, pop some Tylenol and get on with it. Green beer. Green eggs. Hey! Green eggs and ham! Dr. Seuss would be proud of me right now." Rey is too joyful for me this morning or afternoon. Whatever.

I turn around and head back to my bedroom.

"I'll wake you up around five to shower. Don't be a pussy, Katy."

"Time to wake up!" Rey came and jumped on my bed to wake me up. I need to remember to punch her boob.

I groaned, "Go away, Rey."

"No, wake up. We're going out tonight. Wake up. I want to tell you about Carson." Rey slides under the covers with me and tells me all about her night. Between the flirty conversations, the leg touching, and how they ended up coming back to the apartment together.

An hour later she is still telling me about her night. She didn't leave out one detail. I love her, but I could be sleeping. I haven't slept much since we started rehearsal. Between having to be at the theater, classes, and homework, I've had many late nights and many early mornings. I feel like I haven't had any time to rest. I take advantage of my Saturday lazy days.

"Come on, get in the shower. Find something green to wear. I bought us headbands." Of course, she did.

I crawl out of bed and head to the bathroom. I see a washcloth laying in the floor. It instantly came back to me; that belongs Officer Lovely. I hop in the shower and try not to think about last night's incidents. I remember flirting with Mark and then things slowly begin to fade. I remember Officer Lovely but not the conversation. I just remember him being dreamy. Why did I call him Lovely?

I head to my dreaded closet. This is the worst part of my day on the weekends. Unless I'm in my lazy clothes, I have the one outfit I wore last night that makes me actually look presentable. Luckily, for me, I have the St. Patrick's Day t-shirt from last year that I can wear again. I don't have social media so who is going to actually remember?

I find my white t-shirt with my four-leaf clover on it. I dig out some green earrings from my jewelry box, when I lift open the lid I see the photo of me standing in front of the White House. My mood instantly changes. I need to get rid of that picture. I rip the picture out of the box and head back to my closet. I open up a shoe box on my top shelf and shove it in. I slam my closet door. I inhale a deep breath and hold it for a few seconds. My exhale is interrupted by Rey opening up my bedroom door.

"Kat? You ok?"

I exhaled with a sigh, "Yeah. I'm fine." I shake it off and head back over to the vanity. Trying to move on, "So, who's all going tonight? You, me, Carson? Please tell me others are going so I'm not the third wheel."

"Yes, me, you, Mark, Carson. Toby, but Cori has to work, and I think we are meeting some of the crew there," she responds while standing there all fabulous. She's wearing a green tee that reads 'Pinch Me, Kiss Me, Lick Me'. Whore. If only; she is more of a tease. With her looks and personality, she can get any guy she wants but her dad must approve of him or she kicks them to the curb. With both of us growing up with only one parent we bond well on that aspect. I wouldn't date a guy whom my mom wouldn't approve.

With Rey only having a father, my mother has become *our* mother. Rey could call my mom any time of the day if she needed anything. She helped get Rey ready for her first prom, she helped through our hormonal stage all through intermediate school. Through heartbreaks and other issues only *moms* would understand. When we first moved in here, three years ago, my mom helped decorate her room as well as our entire apartment. My mom loves her like her own.

"Does this look ok?" I point to my outfit. My tee and black jeggings with my black flats. Basic. My hair is in its normal state of waves. My makeup is subtle but flashing with green, glittery eye shadow and fake lashes and my 'cat eye' eyeliner over my tattooed eyeliner. It's my signature. Simple with a touch of bold.

"You look great. Let me grab your headband and we can go." She brings back a green headband. Hers has clovers springing from the top, while mine has green cat ears. "Put these on. You look adorable."

"Yes, because adorable has landed me my invisible boyfriend." I roll my eyes, grab my black clutch and out the door we go.

Walking out of the apartment building door, heading north, I see that the bookstore Open sign is still on. "Shit."

"What? What's wrong? What did you forget?" Rey checks me up and down to see what I forgot.

"The bookstore. I was going to apply here."

"This bookstore?" Rey points. "I heard this place was ran by some rich folks that were hard to please. That's why they are always hiring. She grabs my arm without missing a beat and we continue walking.

Maybe that's my sign I don't need a job. I just need to focus on my performance, getting through finals, and focusing on my last year of school. Starting next year, I'll have to start looking for a big girl job. I'll have a degree in political science with a minor in dance. I thought I would become a lawyer one day but the older I get, the more I would like to dance. Sure, there isn't any money in dancing, unless I really do become a stripper, I contemplate.

Rey rattled on about Carson. Carson this. Carson that. We hadn't even made it to the club yet and I was ready to go back home. I shouldn't be like that. I need to be supportive. She's been supportive of all the douchebags I've dated. Even much more when we broke up. I put a smile on my face and open my ears.

The line to the club is wrapped around the block. "Did we not get reservations?!" I yell over the crowd.

"Yes, Mark rented a booth for us to eat first." she looked around for the guys. They were standing at the door waiting for us. Eight o'clock sharp.

We sit down at the booth that Mark rented. It's a nice pub. The booths are hunter green leather that goes well with the mahogany wood walls and dark trim. The bar is all mahogany with red chandeliers giving off dim light. With it being McVey's Irish Pub, St. Patrick's Day is equivalent to the Mexican's Cinco De Mayo parties. There are four leaf clover decorations hanging from the ceilings and about the bar. Green beer is flowing from tap and waitresses are walking around with green Jell-O shots. It's only eight, but I guess there is no rule on what time you can start doing Jell-O shots. The waitress comes to our table to take our order before she can even tell us her name-

"We'll take twelve Jell-O shots," I proclaimed.

"Kat!" Rey responds in surprise.

I nod my head at the waitress in reassurance. She sets twelve down on the table. "That will be twelve dollars."

"I'm going to start a tab with dinner. Put these on mine." I say adamantly. I have no money, but hey, I'll buy shots for everyone all night long. We order a couple pitchers of beer and they seem to disappear quickly.

The green beer continues to flow, the green shots continue to be bought, the flirting becomes heavier. The beat is getting louder and are bodies are getting looser. I grab Mark's hand and we head to the dance floor. He's a good dancer. With being a musical director, I guess one should know how to dance. My arms go above my head and I let my lower half lose control. Mark keeps up with me and the beat. My head is fuzzy and I'm carefree.

"I really like you!" Mark yells over the music.

"I really like me too!" I say laughing back. I do really like Mark, but I'm scared how it will affect our professional relationship. But, at this moment all I can think about is how sexy he looks under these lights and our surroundings. I grab his shirt collar and pull him down to my lips.

The kiss was filled with lust. We were back to back with other people dancing but, in the moment, it is only us on that floor. He grabs the back of my neck and brings his tongue to the back of mine. His other hand wraps around my waist and brings my body pressed against his.

The song begins to die down and a new one starts; our kiss is still going strong. So strong, I'm pretty sure that guy just bumped us on purpose. Mark bites my lower lip and I smile. I have been waiting on that kiss for a long time.

We finally head back to our table. I drink more and more. I'm laughing harder and harder. Rey and I make our jokes about the guys all in flirtatious fun. Mark's hand is placed on my thigh and our body chemistry brings our shoulders closer together.

I haven't had this much fun in a long time. I hardly ever let loose. It seems as if when I do, something usually comes crashing down and I suffer for a while. I'm just not sure if I can handle any more heartache, it's best if I keep this fun, and fun only.

The night comes to an end and I find Rey to drag her home. "I'm going home with Carson. You should go home with Mark!" she yells as if she thinks every idea is a great idea.

"Oh, no. You made me promise you that you'd go home alone. That's what we are going to do. Carson, I'm sorry, but you'll just have to take her to lunch tomorrow or something if you want to see her." I wink at him, grab my clutch and Rey's hand. "Mark, I'll see you Monday morning."

"Kat, I don't remember saying that? I wouldn't have said to take me home. You're drunk, Kat. You don't know." Rey drunkenly rambles on.

She's right, I am drunk. And truth is she didn't say to make sure she got home, but I needed a scape-goat and she's taking one for the team right now. I can't let Mark come home with me. She can be mad at me right now, but she'll understand tomorrow.

We stumble four blocks back home. Laughing and falling over one another. Next thing we know, blue and red lights are flashing at us.

Chapter 4

"Damn it, Kat, what did you do!" Rey yells at me.

"The hell if I know. It's probably your fault. Do you have all of your clothes on?" I look at her body making sure she's appropriate. "Ok, stand up, keep it together. We're fine."

"Miss Cambridge," his voice stops me in my tracks.

"Officer Lovely," I say drunkenly surprised.

"Officer Lovely!" Rey yells. "I heard about you! I heard all—"

I jab her in the ribs with my elbow.

"Actually, it's Officer Lakes," he corrects.

"Lakes! That's it!" Why couldn't I remember that?

"Ladies, you are quite loud out here. We had a complaint called about two drunk girls standing outside the laundry-mat talking loudly for a while now."

I look around, how are we still standing in front of the laundry-mat? I swear we were here twenty minutes ago.

"Miss Cambridge, after last night, I would think you have had enough to drink for a while. You guys need to move it along. I would hate to have to take you with me."

"I'll go wherever you want me to go," Rey tries to flirt. I know that look. I've seen that look a lot on Rey's face.

"Officer Lovely you need to step back," I demand.

"Excuse me?"

"Step back! It's coming!"

"What's coming?" Before I can explain, Rey vomits right there on the sidewalk. "Are you shitting me?" he yells. "What is with you girls and puking?"

"I tried to warn you!" I pull back Rey's hair. "We're fine, Officer, I'll get her home right away."

"Oh, no, you guys are coming with me."

"What! Why? There's no need to take us to jail. We live just a few blocks down the street. I can see it from here!" I help Rey stand up straight and we try to walk around Officer Lakes. "Excuse us, but we'll be fine."

"Get in the car girls." He opens the back door and stands there with his gorgeous blue eyes staring us down. He does a circle in the road and heads back south towards our apartment. "This is ridiculous. You are grown-ups. How do grown-ups throw up so much?"

"Why are you so angry?" I ask him. I told him to back up, it's his own stupidity for not listening.

"I'm not angry. I'm just disappointed I get a call and it's you, again. Drunk, again." He pulls up in front of our apartment. "Here, I'm taking you girls upstairs and cleaning off my shoes, again."

"Sheesh, ok, dad." I smirk. He sure does now how to ruin a buzz. I'm suddenly sober and pissed. I grab my keys out of my purse. "Here," I toss the keys to Officer Lakes, "take your shoes off," I laugh.

He unlocks our street door. I roll my eyes at him as he holds the door open for us. Rey is carrying herself up their stairs while Officer Asshole and I follow.

"Katy, I don't have my keys," Rey realizes.

"Here, I'll get it," Officer Lakes shuffles around us and unlocks our door. Rey and I walk through while he takes off his shoes.

"I'm going to bed. Thanks for not arresting me." Rey quickly trots off down the hallway.

"Is she going to be ok?"

"She'll be fine. Let me get you a rag." I walk to the kitchen to get a rag out of the drawer. I turn on the faucet and dabble some dish soap onto the washcloth. "Here."

He takes the rag from me with a bold look in his eyes. He knows I'm aggravated and from the look in his eyes, he's aggravated too. His eyes are firm but pensive. "Thanks. I have never in my life been puked on and I meet you and this happens to me twice."

"Have you ever thought that maybe people are just that repulsed by you, that they see you and instantly vomit?" I say with a smart tone.

"I haven't before but now I guess I should probably start brushing my teeth more. It seems as soon as I open my mouth, puke comes out of yours." He finishes wiping his shoes down. He starts to walk down the hall. I follow. He throws the soiled rag in the bathroom floor, again.

I turn and go into my bedroom. He stands in my doorway. His black uniform covers his built physique with his belt carrying his equipment around his waist. His badge sits one side of his button-down collared shirt that is clearly covering his bullet proof vest, while on the other side is his gold-plated name tag with 'Officer Lakes' on it.

The heat radiating off his body is intense. I don't know what it is about a man in a police uniform, but I'm suddenly turned on. His cuffs hanging from his strap is enough to make any girls erotic dreams come to life. I'm suddenly finding myself light-headed. I bring my hand to my forehead and try to focus on a counter-point.

"Are you ok?" he asks concerned. "Are you going to throw up now, too?" He takes a step back and puts his arms out in front of him as if he is halting me from moving.

"Relax, I'm fine. I'm just a little light-headed."

"Ok, you sit here, I'll grab you some water." What is it with this guy getting me water? Is this last night playing again in my head? It's supposed to be St. Patrick's Day, not Groundhog Day.

I take my flats off and put my phone on charge. He brings me a bottle of water.

"I was going to bring you a Tylenol, but I didn't want to fondle through your things."

I snarled. "You said fondle."

He rolls his eyes, "Okay, Katy, time to lay down."

"What did you say your name was, Officer Lakes?"

"Chad. Chad Lakes. Well, Officer Chad Lakes. You can call me Lakes. Or Chad. Or Officer Lovely. Whichever you prefer."

"Oh, someone's got jokes!" I snarl. "Alright, Officer Chad, lock the door on your way out. And stop trying to arrest me. You're not very good at this game."

"Katy, you haven't even begun to see that games that I can play."

"Is that a threat or a promise?"

"Goodnight Katy." He heads back down the hallway and I hear the door close behind him.

Sunday morning came quick. Officer Lakes was right, I have a headache. Bastard. I get up and head to the bathroom. While sitting down to pee, I notice the washcloth on the floor. That man really knows how to make my skin crawl. Him coming in my house like he owns the place.

Please. Just throws his rag on the floor like it's his bathroom.

How is it that I have never seen this man before and then two nights in a row he's been in my apartment? He has some nerve stopping us on the street like that. Doesn't he have crimes to solve as opposed to worrying about two drunk girls having a little fun? I guess not. Maybe Middletown needs to step up its crime rates, so Officer Lovely has better things to do than give me shit.

I wash my hands and brush my teeth. I decide I should go ahead and shower. I can't be lazy like I was yesterday. There's things I need to get done. I might even take Mom some lunch. Maybe Rey would like to come, if she's talking to me, of course.

I let the pressure of the warm water hit my head. I tilt my head down and sulk in my dreadful thoughts of having to get a job. I know I should, but I already feel like I don't have any time. Just suck it up, Kat. I can do this. It's only going to be like twenty hours a week if I get one. Twenty hours. That's almost a whole day. Do I really have an entire day to spare dedicated to something other than dance, studies and my free time? How do people do this? I don't think I'm ready for a big girl job. I don't want to give up my freedom. I also don't want to keep taking out student loans just to be able to buy food. Boy, I do like food.

I get out of the shower and get dressed. It's another lazy day for me. It's supposed to be warmer today, so I'm wearing capris, a grey ribbed tank with a blue zip-up hoodie with flip flops. My hair is pulled back in a low ponytail and I'm wearing my glasses.

I normally don't wear glasses or contacts, but with my headache today I don't need any additional strains. I pop a couple of pain pills and chase them with the water bottle Officer Lovely gave me last night.

Why do I keep calling him that? I should call him Officer Lame or Officer Lickmynuts. Only, my goodness, he is handsome. Those eyes could make the moon jealous. I want to run my fingers through his scruffy beard up to his short dark colored hair. Then make my way down the back of his strong toned neck. What is wrong with me?

I know exactly what is wrong with me. I haven't had a boyfriend in a year. I have all this sexual tension built up. The last guy I slept had been over six months ago. He was a potential boyfriend. We had gone out on a few dates, he stayed over a couple of times, he met my friends, then suddenly he was gone. He stopped responding to texts, calls, and he blocked me on social media.

That's when I gave up social media altogether. If people were going to be that way with me, I was going to be that way with everyone else. Also, my mother was always against social media and putting myself out there for anyone to be able to find.

I head downstairs to the sub shop. I walk in to find a short line. I text my mom saying that I'll be there in fifteen minutes. She only lives a few minutes away. I order our sandwiches and head on my way.

Mom lives on the southside of Middletown. It isn't the best place to live in town. She lives in an apartment complex surrounded by rowdy neighbors and thugs hang out on the street in the night. Luckily, she's never had any issues. I don't remember any while growing up there. I can still play my music loudly on the rooftop and no one thinks twice about it. It's like the sound of the train living next to the tracks. You just become used to the sound. Sometimes, I even miss it when it's too quiet.

Why isn't Officer Lakes more concerned about that area as opposed to my area? I'm a big girl, I can handle myself. It's people on the southside the police need to worry about.

Wait, why am I so concerned about where he's concerned about? Why is this bothering me so much? It must be the alcohol clouding my head. I just need to eat and clear my mind. Mom always helps clear my head. She always knows the right thing to say.

I get into my blue, two door Ford Escort. This car is over twenty years old. But It's been well kept. It still has the original radio in it. My mom wouldn't let me change it into a C.D. player. I had to carry a battery-operated stereo with me and turn it up in my back seat. Then it got stolen. I guess there was some crime back when I was younger.

I wonder why I blocked that out. I seem to have blocked a lot out as a child. I remember high school. I remember Rey. I don't remember much else.

A few minutes later I'm on the southside. The homes are close together and my mom's apartment complex sits next to the train tracks. She lives in a two-story brick building with two apartments upstairs and two apartments downstairs. There's a backdoor that has an outdoor staircase that takes you to the roof for maintenance. That's where I liked to spend my alone time. I have come up with my best choreography on that roof.

I walk upstairs to my mom's apartment on the left. I walk into the living room that is connected to the kitchen. It's a worn-down apartment. Mom doesn't seem to mind. She's set in her ways. She has floral furniture with an old wooden box television that sits on the floor. She has an old glass dome clock with a rotating pendulum sitting on her television that chimes every hour. She's had that clock for as long as I can remember. She bought it once while she was on one of her many road trips.

"Mom?"

She walks in the kitchen from the pantry. "Hey sis." The sound of Mom's voice instantly calms any nerves I may have. I'm home.

I walk into the kitchen and set the bag of sandwiches on the counter. Her kitchen has oak cabinets with tan countertops. Her kitchen is decorated in roosters and red accent pieces. There's a window above her sink with hanging red and white checked curtains. There's enough room in her kitchen for a two-person table. She has a rooster cookie jar as her centerpiece. It looks like a kitchen out of a farmhouse magazine. She bought most of it at a thrift store. Mom would never pay full price for anything for herself.

"I got you a turkey and cheese with only lettuce," I inform her as I pull out a paper plate from the cabinet.

"Let me guess, you got yourself only turkey and cheese?"

"Yes, because I'm not a rabbit and I won't eat like one." I laugh. I turn around to sit down and Mom is standing there with her top lip tucked under with her teeth hanging out, and her hands bowed while shaking her butt. "So, you *are* a rabbit after all."

Mom grabs a couple of red plastic cups and brings over the pitcher of tea. We sit down and set our plates. "So how are you, sweetie?"

"I'm ok," I say although I'm lying. I'm not exactly sure what my problem is but I just feel down today. Maybe there's a storm rolling in.

"Why don't I believe you?" She always knows when something is wrong. My face must give it away. I need to work on that. "So, what's really going on?"

I let out a sigh. "I'm not really sure, Mom. I feel overwhelmed. Between the musical, school and I feel like I need to get a job."

"A job? What made you decide that?" she asks inquisitively as she takes a bite of her sandwich.

While growing up, Mom worked as a beautician at the salon down the street. Her clients mostly consist of younger moms and older ladies in the neighborhood. Her busy season is coming to an end now that most of her clients have spent all their tax-return money.

"Well, I opened my closet and realized I wear the same thing over and over. I want to save my loan money for rent for the rest of the summer. I need the extra cash for things like clothes and play money."

"That sounds like a smart decision. What's holding you back? With summer coming up it will keep you busy. You could always pick up more hours if you wanted."

I never thought about summer time. I need something to keep me busy. Last summer I helped with an older lady that was a client of my mom's. She needed help getting groceries and washing her hair every couple of days. It was nothing extravagant, but she paid me fifty dollars a week and that was enough for me to go out to dinner once a week and gas money. It was all that I needed.

"Yeah, I guess you're right. The bookstore that's by the apartment is hiring. I thought about applying there. It's convenient and it can't be that hard to stock books."

"How's the musical going? What about Mark?" she changes the subject. I guess she doesn't care much about me stocking books.

"Mother." I should never have told her about Mark. She met him years ago when I started school. She always thought he would be good for me. Once she found out he was the director she just knew this would be when we finally got together.

"He's fine. We all went out last night. I just don't think I can make another commitment right now. I'm stressed enough as it is, I don't need to feel like I must report to someone all the time. Nor worry about his feelings and if I'm doing everything right as a new girlfriend."

Dating is hard for someone like me. Is he coming over tonight, is he going to make time for me, is he going to be mad if I don't have to see him because I have other things I want to do? I don't want someone to give up on me just because I have things I want or need to do. I would feel like I need to please them as opposed to doing what I need to do.

We continued to chat over lunch. I helped her fold her towels and I headed back to town. I feel like I need to go to the bookstore immediately before I change my mind.

I park behind our apartment building and walk around the block. As I approach the store I look up to see the sign 'Pond's Paperbacks'. The help wanted sign was still in the windows and the hours on the door showed they were open from noon to five o'clock today. That didn't seem too horrible of hours. If I worked on Sunday's I would still be able to do homework Sunday night. Through the week they open at nine in the morning and close at seven in the evening. It's not like I had to travel far. It took a whole minute from my door to theirs. It's perfect really.

I walk in and the door chimes. There's a few wing-backed chairs with ottomans, a sofa and a loveseat. There were some high-top tables with directors' chairs next to the both walls. It looked like a living room. It was cozy. The aisles of books were perpendicular to the walls. The counter where the register sits was to the left of the store in alignment of the front door. There was an espresso machine on the counter behind the register.

"How come I never knew they had coffee there?" I say quietly to myself. I walk over to the counter where there is an older woman probably in her middle to late fifties. She must own the place. She was shorter with sandy blonde permed hair. She was wearing a pink blouse with a black skirt and heels. I really hope I don't have to wear heels here. A shift on my feet in heels would be a nightmare. I already havr nightmares, I didn't need to live one as well.

"Hi, can I help you?" she says politely.

"Yes, hi. I'm wondering if I can have an application, please?"

"Yes," she says while looking me up and down. She grabs one from under the counter and I grab a pen from the cup next to the register.

I walk over to the high-top table and fill out my application. It asks for my availability. I can work every night, but I have rehearsal until three o'clock for the next week. I wonder if that will hurt my chances? The more I worry, the more I realize that I want this job. I'll just talk to her, calm down Kat. Once I'm finished filling out this application, in which ninety percent I lied on, I walk back over.

"All done?" she asks surprised.

"Yes, ma'am. I would just like to say that I'm currently rehearsing for a musical at Midtown and after the first of April, I will be available every day after noon. I only have classes from eight o'clock am to eleven fifty. And next week is spring break so I will have rehearsals in the morning but be free in the afternoon as well."

"Katy, is it?"

"Yes, Katy Cambridge. It's nice to meet you." I extend my arm to shake her hand. She looks at it and ignores my request. Bitch.

"Ok, Katy. I see you go to Midtown? That's…" she stalls to find the word, "local." She says as if she's shaming me and the school. "But, I think that would be ok. It keeps me from having to be here all day, every day. I only have one other employee, Andrea, at the moment, but she goes to Rivot and can only work on Friday and Saturday. And you girls would rotate every other Sunday. So, that will leave your hours to be one to seven with a thirty-minute lunch, Tuesday, Wednesday, Thursday, both of you girls will work Saturday. We will split the shift on Sunday. Then we are closed on Monday. So, some weeks that would give you five days a week until I can get someone else hired. But you would still have every Friday off. How does that sound?"

"That sounds good to me, when would you like me to train?" I say with excitement.

"How about now? Can you do it now?"

I had to think for a second, "Yes, I don't have anything going on the rest of the afternoon. I was just plan- "

"Great," she interrupts. "I'm not too concerned about your personal life, I just need you to work so I can go home."

Stunned at her ability to be rude to a stranger, I apologize "Sorry, I didn't mean to- "

"No need to apologize but now you know. If you want to walk around here I'll show you how to work the register. It's quite simple. It's all touch screen so if you can read, you can do this job. You scan the books they want to purchase. You hit total. You then hit cash or credit. We do not accept checks. If someone wants to return something, you hit return, it will ask if they have the receipt, you hit yes or no, if yes, scan the barcode on the bottom of the receipt, if no, scan the barcode on the book. It will you give you the amount to give back. We do not return the money on cards, it's only cash. Think you can handle it?"

"Well, I can read, so yes."

"Good. Now the espresso machine."

She goes on talking about the espresso machine and how I need to make sure I wash and sanitize all the dishes and utensils used. We don't sell fresh food, only snacks and water so I need to make sure all of those remain stocked. I must make sure I vacuum and wash off the tables. I will have to set the alarm, I will have a key and to make sure I turn off the open sign. I will never open, so I don't have to worry about making drawers, I just have to worry about printing of the end of day report and putting the money in the slot of the safe underneath the register. I feel like she is giving a lot of responsibility to someone she doesn't even know. In fact, I don't even know her name.

"I'm sorry, but I don't remember your name?" I say embarrassed. Maybe she did tell me, but I must have been in my own world.

She laughs, "I'm sorry, I'm just excited to have someone who wants to work."

It was the first time I saw her lighten up and put a smile on her face since I have been here. Rey was right, no wonder why they have a high turn-over rate. I bet she is hard to work for. I wonder if she's always this miserable and unfriendly or if she is just stressed about having to cover all the shifts until now. I can't imagine being woeful about having to be here. This is the most solemn place I've been in a while. It's quiet like a library. There's no gossip, no loud music, nothing but mature adults reading mature books in a mature setting. I can't believe in the three years I've lived upstairs that I had never been in here before now. Especially not knowing there is a coffee station in here. Is there not a sign on the front window? I don't remember seeing one. I bet it would bring in a lot more customers if people knew there was an espresso machine. That's how the bigger bookstore chains get a lot of their draw these days since print books are being replaces with electronics.

"Anyways, I'm Kathy Lakes."

"Lakes?" I hear the bell chime at the front door, I turn to see who's coming in.

It's him.

Chapter 5

"Oh, excuse me for a moment, my son is here." She walks around the counter to greet him.

Son? Officer Lakes is my boss' son. Now I can see where he gets his attitude. What is happening in this world? Three years I have never been in here, in three years I have never seen this man, and now three days in a row I've run into him.

He sure does look sexy in his everyday attire. She's wearing athletic pants with a hoodie, a ball cap and tennis shoes. It took me a second to make sure it was him. I hadn't ever seen him out of his police uniform and I am taken back by his appeal. How can anyone be this tall and sexy? His father must be tall.

"Last night was calm around here, except for some drunk chicks walking home from the bar," he says to his mother as he glares into my direction.

"Hmm. Well, I don't think I have to be too concerned with any drunk chicks breaking into my store and stealing a safe. If they can't walk, they surely can't carry a safe and not get caught."

Stealing a safe? Did this place get robbed? How do I not know these things? I've been walking these streets for years now and suddenly places are being robbed? No wonder why Officer Lakes is creeping these streets.

"Excuse me," I say. "Did you say robbed?"

"That's not going to scare you away is it?" Kathy asks.

"Um- "

"Before you say you don't want this job, let me tell you what actually happened," she tries to negotiate.

"Job? You're working here now?" Officer Lovely asks.

"Yes."

"Ha. Of course, you are," he says.

"Wait, do you two know each other?" Kathy wonders aloud.

"Yes, mother. She is one of the drunk girls who stumbles outside of your window at night."

"Officer Lakes!"

"Chad. His name is Chad. And you're a 'drunk chick?'" Kathy catechizes.

"Not normally." I try to weasel my way out of this one. This is just what I want; my new petulant boss to already have an undesirable observation of who I really am. "This weekend was a special occasion."

"I'm not sure it being the weekend classifies it being an 'occasion'" he uses his fingers to mock me.

"That's enough you two. If this is going to be a problem between you two, Katy, maybe this isn't going to work out, after all," Kathy states.

"No, mother. There won't be any issues." Chad defends me. I'm utterly surprised by this. As cocky and arrogant as he is maybe he has a heart beneath his chilling exterior. That, or he has an alternative motive.

"Katy, I do believe that's it for today. I will see you Tuesday?" Kathy asks to make sure I'm still on board.

"Yes, Tuesday. And thank you again." I walk out the door and head back to my apartment. I walk inside to see Rey sitting on the couch doing homework. "Hey, you."

"Hey." Rey is unusually calm. Something must be going on in that head of hers.

"What's with you?"

"Nothing, really. Just hating literature at the moment. And Carson."

"What? Why?" I walk over to the fridge to grab a bottle of water.

"He hasn't called today. He must be pissed that I didn't go home with him," Rey glares in my direction.

Defensively I throw my hands up, "Hey now, I was in no shape to walk home alone. I needed you."

"I know, I know. Sorry. I just wonder what's going on with him."

"He's probably just hungover, Rey. He'll call. Boyfriends always call," I say giving her a hard time.

"Go away," she laughs.

"Oh, and Rey, it's spring break. Put the book down." I tease because she has clearly forgotten.

"Shit!" she laughs as she tosses the book on the coffee table.

I walk down the hallway to my room to change my clothes. I can't decide what book I'm going to start tonight. I haven't really had much time to read one but seeing it's spring break I should have some spare time to start one. Well, I did have time before I decided to get a job. Maybe I shouldn't start a book. I could practice my lines. Nah, I don't want to do that. Maybe go to the roof and dance. Yeah, that's what I'll do.

I undress and put on my leotard, sweater and leggings. I'm most comfortable with this look. I really feel like I'm in the movie Flashdance. I feel cute in this and that's all that matters. I leave my hair back in a low ponytail and grab my battery-operated C.D. player. I hear a knock on my door. Rey must be bored.

"Come in," I yell while I'm digging in my closet for my radio.

"Katy?" I hear his voice. I turn around quickly.

"Chad? What are you doing here?" Why is he here? I'm not drunk. I'm not walking the streets causing a ruckus; I'm just minding my own business.

"I just wanted to apologize. I should clarify I had no intention to extort you in front of my mother. I shouldn't have said what I said about you drinking. I didn't realize my mother was going to take it the way she did."

"Oh. Well, thanks." We stand there in awkward silence. What now? A few moments pass as I get lost in his eyes. "Are you not working tonight?"

He continues to stand by the bedroom door as I sit on the bed to pull up my leggings. "No, not tonight. I'm typically off on Sunday's.

"Oh, that's nice." This is weird. Do I continue the conversation? Do I tell him I'm busy? Why would he just show up?

"Yeah. Well it looks like your busy, so I'll go. I just wanted to clear that up."

I stand up from my bed to walk him out, "Well, thank you. I appreciate that." We just stand there looking at each other. Why is this so odd? It's probably because I'm sober or it's because I barely know him and he's in my apartment.

"Yeah. Alright." He turns to walk away but suddenly stops himself. He turns around, "missed opportunities."

"Huh?"

He steps forward and grabs the back of my neck and pulls me in closer to him. He brings his lips to mine. I am at a standstill. I should probably kiss him back.

My mouth opens in full embrace. He puts his other hand on the small of my back and brings my body closer to his. Our heads tilt back and forth as he grazes his tongue against mine. A few seconds pass and he slowly pulls his lips away. I stand there in awe and shock.

"I've been wanting to do that since Friday." He turns around and walks out.

I stand there astonished and speechless. Do I go after him?

I make the decision to step out of my room and look down the hall. He must know I'm watching him because he turns around.

"I'll talk to you later, Katy."

"How? You don't even know my number?"

"I know where you live." He walks turns and walks out of the apartment.

Rey comes running down the hall. "What the hell was that?'

"I don't even know. He kissed me."

"What! Why? Wait? I'm confused."

"Yeah, me too." I turn around and walk back to my bed and grab my C.D. player.

I need to dance this off. I head to the roof and turn on the music. I try to clear my fuzzy head but right now, dancing isn't even fixing this. I would try to run it off, but I don't run.

Why am I so hung up on this? So, he kissed me? So, what? I've been kissed before. Never in that matter. Not even sure it's ever been that passionate. There's so much animosity between us, I never realized it was tension. Get it together. You're fine. It's a kiss.

Oh, but it was a good kiss. My soul drops to my stomach at the thought of it. Every bit of stress I had, was gone when he held and kissed me. It was just what I needed to get over this slope I've been in. Now, I feel like I'm on top of the world. Maybe that's why I can't concentrate on dancing; because I am already relieved of the burden I was carrying.

I decide to do a couple skills, some leaps, spins, and a few stretches. I begin to feel better and continue to practice my routine for next weekend.

I can't believe the play is almost here. I've been working on this piece for almost four months now. I've spent many hours choreographing and perfecting the dances. Count after count, beat after beat, spin after spin. Rey has been a lifesaver, when I get dancers block, Rey steps in and knows just the right transition from piece to piece.

I've had enough of the dancing for the day. I pack up my radio and head back to the apartment. I notice a black SUV in the alley, I wonder if that is Kathy's vehicle? It's a black Escalade with black rims. I notice an older man, tall, skinny with a scruffy beard carrying a black bag. He must be Chad's father, they resemble one another. I wonder if he is conceded like his son or if he's that's where he gets what little heart he has, from.

A few days past with zero excitement; wake up and dance, go to sleep, wake up and dance, go to work, go to sleep. Mark is awkward because I won't go to dinner with him. Spring break is almost over and hasn't been all it's cracked up to be. I haven't been drinking so I haven't had any run-ins with the law nor has he come into the bookstore. I haven't heard from Chad since he kissed me and left.

The job is easy. Stock, check out customers, stock, check out customers. Life has become repetitive and boring. Kathy has hired one more person, so I won't be working five days a week after all. Her name is Samantha. She seems to be nice. She's studying law at Rivot. Kathy must have an infatuation with Rivot or a loyalty, whichever.

Sam is from Korea and is working on her citizenship to be able to practice law in the States. She came to the U.S. when she was fourteen with her family, so she has spent time learning the language and culture over here. She's very modern in style. She wears red eccentric glasses that form well with her heart-shaped face. She has a fixation with scarves. Every outfit I've seen her in she has a scarf around her neck.

I'm about to lock the door when I see a police car pull up. "Great," I say aloud. I turn off the open sign when I hear Officer Lakes.

"Hold on, don't lock it," he demands.

"Um, ok." Is this how this is going to pan out. I'm going to have him as a boss, too?

"Step back, don't go in there." He draws his gun and holds it close to his chest.

"What the hell are you doing?"

"Step. Back." he says adamantly. A second cop car pulls up and an officer jumps out with his hand on his pistol ready to draw. "Police! If you in there come out now with your hands up! We have the K9 in the car! Come out now!"

Kathy comes running from behind me, "Katy, oh thank God you're okay!"

"What is going on?" I ask inquisitively.

"You need to go straight to your apartment, right now!" Kathy is yelling at me.

"But- "

"Now!" she exclaims.

I'm not going to argue with her. I head to the street door of my apartment only to be greeted by Rey.

"What the hell is going on? I saw the cops from the window," she states.

"Turn around, go back upstairs."

"Why? What's going on?" Rey questions.

"Damn it, Rey, just do what I say." I put one hand on her shoulder and the other on her waist and turn her back-around.

"What is your problem?" she asks while stomping up the stairs. She opens the apartment door and I shut it behind me.

"Sheesh. Will you just listen instead of me having to treat you like a child?"

"No. In fact, now I want my blankey," she says in her smart-aleck tone of voice.

"There's been a robbery at the bookstore. Well, it's actually happening right now." I'm trying to catch my breath. What if I was in there? Why is this bookstore a target? Are the Lakes into something dangerous? What did I get myself into?

Rey must have read my mind, "No shit? What did you get yourself into?"

"Yeah, no shit. This is insane. I was just locking up the doors and Chad comes-

"Chad, eh? He was coming?" Rey says laughing.

"Will you be an adult for two seconds?"

"Ok, I'm sorry, go ahead," she says with a smile on her face.

"Anyways, Chad comes running to the store and whips out his gun talking about the K9 and shit. I was trying to find out what was going on and Mrs. Lakes was all like 'I'm glad you're okay but get your ass upstairs', kind of thing. "Then I had to argue with you and now here we are."

"So, you don't know anything then?" Her tone is about to piss me off. She can't take anything seriously.

"No, asshole. I don't know anything."

"Well, what good are ya?" She's in a playful mood.

"What is with you? Why are you all…chipper?" I ask. She's just smiling and laughing and here I am worried about my life in danger.

"I just got laid," she says with a smile on her face.

"Unbelievable. Here I am, almost murdered by some bad guy and all you can talk about is sex. And for the record, of course, you did, slut." There's a knock on the door. I turn to open it. On the other side of the door stands Officer Lovely in his uniform looking delicious. He looks like he hasn't shaved in a few days which makes me swoon over him even more. I have to refrain from chewing on his neck right now.

"Katy, are you ok?' he says frantically checking me up and down.

"Yes, I'm fine. What happened down there?"

"I need to bring you into the station for questioning," he says.

"Questioning? What for?" I ask surprised.

"It's just routine. I need you to come with me.'

I look at Rey in disbelief.

"You'll be ok. You get to ride in a cop car!" she says.

"Seriously, you're such an asshole." I say to her as I walk out the door.

We get downstairs and he opens up the back-passenger door.

"You've got to be kidding me?" I ask laughing.

"I'm not. Get in," he says firmly in his cop voice.

I huff and slide into the back seat.

"Buckle up."

"Yes, officer." I say in my smart-aleck tone. Everyone else gets to be a jerk today, why can't I?

"I've been wanting to do this for a while now," he laughs as he shuts the door.

What a dick.

Driving to the station there's an awkward silence. I can't handle it.

"So, are you going to tell me what's going on?"

"The detective on the case will explain everything when we get to the station, Katy."

"You can call me Kat."

"Kat? Like a kitty cat?" he laughs.

"Yes, like a kitty cat." What is the deal with all of these smart-aleck's in my life. I need new friends. Friendly friends. Polite friends. Then I would be bored. I guess I'll keep these assholes around.

"I'll stick with Katy," he says.

We arrive at the station and he comes around to let me out of the car. I feel like I'm a ten-year-old again with my mom having child lock on the windows and doors. "Thank you."

"Yep." His persona has changed. He walks me into the station and we are buzzed in the door. He walks me into an interrogation room. The walls are grey with a two-sided mirror overlooking the room. There's a single white industrial table sitting in the middle of the room. There are two padded chairs sitting across from one another. I stand there looking at Chad.

"What the hell is this?" I ask.

"The detective will be in momentarily," he responds.

Enters a man about six feet tall, with a receding hair line with a bushy gray beard. He's wearing khakis with a blue, collard button-down shirt that covers his beer gut. He must not be out in the field much. He looks like a desk guy. He has a gun clipped onto one side of his belt while his badge is on the other side.

"Katy, this is Detective Marshall. He has a few questions for you," Officer Lakes states.

"Hi, Katy. Take a seat." His voice is deep and scratchy. He must be a smoker.

I take a seat and fold my hands on the table. The room is cold and uncomfortable. I've never been in one of these before. I've only been in a police station once and that was when I was little.

"Alright, let's get started," he says as he takes a seat across from me. "Miss Cambridge. Before we start I just wanted to let you know you are being recorded. You understand that you have the right to remain silent and you have the right to end this questioning whenever you feel like it."

"Wait, am I under arrest?" I ask in shock. Why am I being brought into the station? Why am I being read my rights? Do they think I had something to do with this? Why didn't Chad warn me?

"No. You are simply being questioned. You have the right to leave whenever you want. Officer Lakes will take you back home. OK?" he asks.

"Yes."

"Now, Miss Cambridge, you work at 'Pond's Paperback, correct?"

"Yes."

"How long have you worked there?"

"Um, I started this past Tuesday. So, four days."

"And from my understanding you live above the building, yes?"

"I live above the sandwich shop next to the bookstore, yes."

"Have you noticed any unusual behavior around your apartment building?"

"Unusual? No. Just typical every day, normal routine activity," I said.

"What would you describe as usual?" Detective Marshall inquires while scratches his beard.

"Students and young adults walking up and down the strip. People sitting outside restaurants having conversations, while others are carrying shopping bags enjoy themselves. It's a friendly atmosphere."

"So, what are you saying it's unusual to see middle aged people walking around?" asking as if he's trying to suggest something.

"It's pretty common to see to see middle aged people to be walking around. A lot of the students' parents visit quite often. It's usually very active on the strip."

I love where I live. There's small unique, eccentric shops and little restaurants that have outdoor seating. The rent is decent for its location. We really lucked out when I saw the ad at the sandwich shop one day. I called Rey and the next day we moved in.

"Now, Miss Cambridge you have an active alley behind your apartment. Have you noticed anything unusual behind your building?" he asks.

"Honestly, my bedroom is facing the strip. My roommates room is facing the alley. She would have more information on that than I do. We have a kitchen window, but I rarely look out of it. I know there's delivery trucks in and out of there, but I don't know any specific days."

"Understandable. Now, Miss Cambridge, what's your schedule like?"

"My schedule? My work schedule you mean?" I ask confused.

"Yes," he replies.

"I work Tuesday, Wednesday, Thursday, and we rotate Sundays. I work one o'clock to close; which is seven o'clock. But this is my just my first week." Which might be my last week, I mutter to myself.

"What do you do in the meantime? Are you a student?"

"Yes. I attend Midtown. I have class every day, followed by rehearsal. Then I go to work or come home." I have a pretty, simple routine. I'm easy to find if someone needed me.

"Rehearsal?" he asks.

"Yes, I'm in the Midtown Drama that's being presented tomorrow night," I say with a pep in my tone.

"You sound excited about this?" he notices.

"Yes, very much. We've all been working on this for months." More like working night and day preparing for this weekend. Between building the set, choreographing the dances, writing lyrics for the songs, the entire cast has been busy working on this drama.

"That's great. So, let's review your day, today. Seeing that it's Thursday, did you go to class this morning?"

"Yeah, I had class at eight a.m." All of my classes start at eight. My mom always said get your priorities done early so you can play in the day. "Then I went to rehearsal from ten to twelve. On Monday's and Wednesday's, I only have one on hour class, then Tuesday's and Thursday's I have a two, one-hour classes. Then my rehearsal counts as a two-hour class. But since we have the play coming soon, on Monday's and Wednesday's, I go to the auditorium to practice my routines before the other student's get there."

"Routines?" he asks.

I'm not sure what this has to do with any of the robbery, but I answer. "Yes, I'm a dancer in the play."

"Ah. Okay, sorry to derail here, let's get back to the investigation. Did you notice anything tonight when you were closing up? Any noises, strange customers? Notice any vehicles surrounding the place?"

"No. Nothing out of the ordinary for *me*. But like I said, this is only day three for me. The last customer I had was at six-thirty. I restocked the fridge and vacuumed. So, if there were any strange noises, I honestly wouldn't have noticed."

I'm suddenly scared. Did someone come in the backdoor when I was vacuuming? How did they get in? Did Kathy leave it unlocked when she left? Wait, she went out the front door. I double checked to make sure it was locked when I left. It was locked. So, how could someone have gotten in? Did they lock it behind them?

I can't take it. "Was someone in there when I was there?"

Both men look at each other. There's hesitation.

Chad looks at me, "Yes. We have surveillance cameras hooked up to our phones. We can see everything that goes on in the store. A tall, thin, white male came in when you started to vacuum. The video shows he ran out the back door when I pulled up."

My stomach dropped. I feel sick. I feel violated. How long were they watching me? What were they planning to do? I'm suddenly scared for my life. There's someone creeping around, and I live right there.

"Miss Cambridge, are you ok?" Detective Marshall asks. I must have gone pale because all of my energy has transferred to my stomach.

"I've seen that look before." Chad says. "Get her a trash can. Now."

Chad looks around and finds one in the corner. He slides it next to me just in the nick-of-time. I hurl over and vomit in the trash can. The sounds I make, alone, make me sick. It's quite embarrassing, really.

"Get her some water and a paper towel," Detective Marshall tells Chad.

Chad comes back a few moments later. My head is still in the trash can spewing up what I have left in my body. Chad kneels next to me to hand me the paper towel.

"Thank you," I say while wiping my face. "I'm sorry, but this is a little overwhelming for me. Do you know who it was? What does he want? Why me?" I say looking back and forth at both men.

Detective Marshall responds, "Unfortunately, no. We don't know who it is. This is the second time in a very short amount of time there's been a break-in. Only, they aren't breaking in. They are coming in while the store is open. There's have a security camera in the alley, but the vehicle doesn't have plates on it. That's why I asked if you had seen any suspicious behavior out back."

Suddenly the thoughts of seeing the black escalade pops into my mind. "Wait. Do we know what kind of vehicle it is?"

"A black Escalade," Chad states.

I suddenly feel sick again. I bring the paper towel to my face and try to contain composure. I inhale and exhale.

"Katy, what do you know?" Chad can tell by the look on my face that I know something.

I exhale, "I've seen a black Escalade. I was dancing on the roof earlier this week. I heard someone walking on the gravel. I over-look the side of the building and notice a man carrying a black duffle bag getting into the vehicle. I just assumed it was your father, Chad."

Both men look at each other.

"Can you describe him?" Detective Marshall asks.

"Yes, he's tall. Has darker hair. Skinny. An older man. I thought he looked like an older version of you, Officer Lakes. He was built the same as you," I recall.

"Ok, Miss Cambridge, that's enough for today. I think we have all the information we need," Detective Marshall says trying to end our conversation.

"Wait. You guys are just going to send me home now knowing there's someone on the loose and was fifteen feet away from possibly murdering me?" I ask shocked with a tremor in my voice.

"Officer Lakes will take you home and make sure you get inside safely. I appreciate your cooperation during this interview." Detective Marshall stands up and reaches for my hand. "Eh, I better not," he laughs. "We'll talk soon."

He walks out of the room and I sit and stare at the concrete wall.

"Katy, are you okay?" Officer Lakes asks.

"Am I okay? Am I okay! I could have died tonight if you hadn't of gotten there in time. I'm terrified right now. And now you guys just send me on my way." I throw my hands up in the air, waving. "This man, whoever he is, knows who I am, now!" I yell.

"Ok, breathe. And try not to puke again," he smirks.

"This isn't funny, Chad! How am I supposed to sleep tonight knowing there's a man loose out there? What about Rey? I have to tell her. We walk up and down those sidewalks multiple times a day. We take our trash around back to that dumpster. How do you expect me to just live normally after this?" I notice myself talking hurriedly.

"Look, I know you're scared. Rightfully so. But, I promise you we are doing everything we can," he reconfirms. "We are just a phone call away. And, I'm doing extra patrol. So, if you need anything they will dispatch me out, and I can be there in no time. You're not looking too good, let's get you home."

The car ride home is silent. I'm looking out the window noticing everything going on. Looking at faces walking up and down the street seeing if I recognize anyone. The area is well lit but that doesn't mean the perpetrator isn't walking around in everyday attire.

We pull back up to my apartment. I exhale. I didn't even realize I was holding my breath. Chad walks around and opens my door, which is again, the back-passenger door. He thinks he's funny or he's just trying to lighten the mood. Neither of us say anything. Chad walks me upstairs and I open my door.

The first thing I see is Marks face.

Chapter 6

We walk in as Mark gets up and walks to me wrapping me in his arms. "Mark, what are you doing here?" I say trying to breathe from his suffocation.

"Rey text me."

I glare in her direction. She snickers.

"I'm glad you're ok. Do you need anything? Are you hungry?" he asks.

"No, dad, I'm fine." I say fiercely to get him to understand he's being overbearing at the moment.

Chad clears his throat in annoyance.

"Oh. Mark, this is Officer Lakes," I say annoyed as well.

"Officer Lakes?" Chad looks at me firmly.

"Sorry, I mean Chad." What the hell is his problem?

"Thank you, Officer for making sure she was safe," he says looking at Chad. Mark sticks his arm out to shake Chad's hand. Chad looks extremely agitated now. He takes a good look at Mark as if he's disapproving of him.

I step in, "Mark, give me a second, I'm going to walk Chad out." I close the door behind me as Chad makes his way down the stairs.

"Hey, Chad," I say stopping him. "Thank you." I say sincerely.

"Hey, Kat, you're welcome," he says with a smile. He walks out, locks and closes the door behind him.

I stand there in silence and guilt. Why do I feel guilty? Chad isn't my boyfriend, I've kissed him once. Mark isn't my boyfriend, but I do make-out with him quite a bit. Other than that, I'm single. I'm just little ol' single Kat. Who, up until today, had a pretty, boring life.

I go into the apartment to see Rey, Carson and Mark sitting on the couch laughing. I get hounded with questions but too tired to go into detail. The thunder outside becomes so loud I end up speaking louder. I didn't know it was going to rain tonight. Sometimes I feel like I live in Seattle, not Middletown.

I fill Rey in on how we need to be more careful walking around and to be aware of our surroundings until the Mystery Man is caught.

"This is just bizarre. So bizarre that I need to go to bed now. Let's go, Carson." Rey stands up followed by Carson. "I'm glad you're ok," for once she sounds sincere.

"Thanks, Rey. You two have fun," I say with a wink.

They walk down the hall and it leaves me sitting on the ottoman and Mark sitting on the couch. "Well, I better head out, too," Mark says standing up. "If you need anything at all, you have my number. Try to get some rest we have a big day ahead of us tomorrow."

Oh, shit. Tomorrow is the big day. The day I have been preparing for. My mind is nowhere near where it should be. I need to get some rest. I'm not sure how, but I need to try. Then my mind goes somewhere it shouldn't.

"Wait, Mark." He turns around. "Will you stay with me tonight? I don't feel like being alone."

Mark looks at his watch, then looks back at me. He lets out a sigh, "Yes, of course."

I lock the door and turn out the lights. We walk down the hall to my bedroom. I can hear Rey giggling. She better knock that shit off, I need to rest.

I grab a pair of pajamas out of my drawer and head to the bathroom to change and brush my teeth. I can't believe my day. It makes me wonder what the Lakes are really into? Are they part of the mafia? They've targeted the bookstore for a reason. What's the reason?

I walk back into my bedroom to see Mark stripping down to his boxers. I didn't realize he was so fit. His abdomen is sculpted with his biceps cut. His body is slick. It makes me wonder if he is a secret swimmer.

"Are you ok?" He caught me staring.

"Yes, sorry. It's been a rough day. Don't take this the wrong way, but I just need to be held tonight. As much as your body makes me want to do other things, I need to sleep," I say still looking at his abs.

"Don't worry, I'm just as exhausted. I can't wait for this play to be over. It's wearing me down more than it should," he confesses.

We climb into bed and he wraps his arm around me. I instantly fall asleep.

"Sweetie, are you ok?" Curly Carol asks.

She must see me crying. "I don't know where my daddy went." She grabs my hand.

"Let's go look for him."

She walks me around the restaurant looking for Daddy. "He might be in the potty," I say.

"How about you come home with me and we'll try to call your dad when we get home," she tells me.

"Okay." I grab Kitty Kat and grab Curly Carol's hand.

I get in the backseat of Carol's blue car. The car has no top, so my hair is blowing in my face a lot. Daddy would like this. He would laugh at me. I hope Daddy is okay. Curly Carol turns the music on and starts to sing. I start to sing, too. She's pretty. She has her sunglasses on, I need some sunglasses.

It's getting dark outside. Curly Carol pulls over and hits a button. A weird noise starts and then there's a roof on the car. How cool. Carol smiles at me.

"Why don't you lay down and take a nap. I'll wake you up when we get somewhere warm." I am very sleepy. And there's a blankie right there.

I grab it and snuggle up real tight. I really like Curly Carol. I miss Daddy. I miss Mommy. It's starting to rain and thunder. Boom. Boom. It sounds like drums. Boom. Boom.

I wake up to Carol carrying me in her arms. I open my eyes and we are walking into a brick building. I see cops. Cops with shiny buttons on their shirts.

"Hi, I'm the one who called about the little girl," Carol tells the woman behind the window.

"Yes, Officer Richman will be right with you. Have a seat," the lady working the window tells Carol.

We sit down, with my head still on Carol's shoulder. She pats me on the back.

"We're okay, baby. We just have to talk to the nice man. He's going to see if he can find your Daddy."

The door opens, "Ms. Cambridge, if you will come on back—"

We stand up and follow the police man to the other side of the door. We sit down in a chair next to a desk.

"And who do we have here?" the officer asks me.

"Katy."

"That's a very nice name. Katy, do you have a last name?"

"Westlake."

"Katy, can you tell me your daddy's name?"

"Jason."

"Good job. Do you know your address?"

"455 E. Douglas, Apartment C, Middletown, Connecticut."

"You are doing great. Do you know your phone number?" he asks.

I look down, "No, I don't know my phone number."

"That's okay, sweetie," Carol tells me while patting my leg.

"Okay, Katy, I have some colors right over there at that table, can you go color me a picture?" the officer asks. "I'll hang it right up here on my filing cabinet."

"Okay. I walk over to the table and find some crayons in a cup. I flip through the coloring book and find a page with a kitten on it. I think this is perfect to give the police man."

Carol talks talk to Police Man Richman for a little while. I hear them whispering but can't understand what they are saying.

I finish my coloring page and get up out of my chair. "I'm all done."

"Oh, let me take a look at that." *He takes my colored kitten,* "That's very pretty. I'll hang this right here. Thank you very much, Katy."

"You're welcome."

"Okay, Katy, we are ready to go home now." *Carol picks me back up.* "Thank you, Officer Richman. I'll be in touch."

We walk back outside to the car. "I'm sleepy, Carol, are we almost home?"

"We'll be there shortly. You just get snuggled up back there and I'll let you know when we get home. Okay, sweetie?"

I nod my head, "Night, night, Carol."

"Night, night, sweetheart."

After dosing off, Carol wakes me up and tells me we are at her house. It's a white house with blue shutters. There's flowers in the front yard. I like Carol's house. It's pretty. It's much nicer than the apartment I live in with Daddy. I really need to potty.

"I need to go potty," *I tell her.*

"Come on in, Sis. We'll get you all set up."

She takes my hand and opens the white fence up to her house. She opens the door and it smells nice. It smells like flowers. My house doesn't smell like flowers. My house smells like the school bathroom.

"Ok, sweetie, right down the hallway is the bathroom. Yell for me if you need me."

I walk down the hallway and use the potty. I come out and see a pretty bedroom with flowers on the table. That bed looks comfy. I don't have a bed at home, I usually fall asleep on the couch watching cartoons. Daddy puts a blankie on me when I go to sleep. I used to have a bed, but Daddy said we had to sell it. It's okay. Sometimes Daddy lets me snuggle with him.

"I'm in here, Katy." *I follow the sound of her voice to the kitchen. She has little table. I like it.* "Katy, take a seat for me. I'm going to try to call your daddy.*

"Okay," *I say smiling back. She's so nice. I really, really like her.*

"How about we get you ready for bed and I'll try to call your daddy while you're sleeping?" *I nod, and we walk down to the bedroom with the flowers.* "How about this room? It's pretty like you are. I'll get you a shirt to sleep in, okay?"

I change my clothes and she picks them up and takes them out of room. She comes back in smiling. She tucks me and Kitty Katy in real tight. "Now you try to get some sleep. I'm going to go call your daddy and see what we can do."

"Miss Carol? Will you tell Daddy I said goodnight?" I ask her.

"I sure will, sweetie." She walks out of the room and I hear her make a call. I close my eyes.

I wake up and hear Daddy. He's yelling. "No!"

"You can't just leave her here, she's your daughter!"

"Yes, I can!" The door slams. Boom.

I sit straight up in the bed. I'm sweating. I'm breathing heavy. It's still raining, I can hear the thunder. I feel the sinking of the bed from Mark. It's been awhile since I've had someone in my bed. I carefully crawl out of bed, trying not to wake him. I head to the kitchen to get a drink of water.

I open up the fridge and grab a bottle of water. I walk over to the sink and look out the window. I see a cop car drive down the alley. I wonder if it's Chad? I look at the time and it's six-thirty a.m. It's time to start my day. I have class and then one last rehearsal. I need to shower and wake up Mark.

I take a shower and get dressed as quietly as possible but not quiet enough.

"Good morning, beautiful," I hear.

Ugh. Cheesy. "Sorry, I was trying to be quiet."

'You're fine." He looks at the clock. "I need to get up anyways."

He crawls out of bed and gets dressed. I let my hair air dry into its natural curls while dab on some foundation and mascara.

"So, I will see you at nine?" Mark asks.

"Yes, I'll be there right after class. Do you want me to bring you anything to eat or drink?"

"No, I'll be ok. Maybe. I don't know. Just check your phone, I might decide I need something," he chuckles.

"Okay, come on, I'll walk out with you," I say. We head downstairs to leave. I turn right to go to my car and he turns left to head home. I take a few steps before I see Chad staring at me. He's standing there in his charcoal Nike athletic pants and his black Nike athletic dry-fit t-shirt with his arms crossed leaning up against a black Lincoln MKZ. My gosh he's edible. His fierce blue eyes are burning a laser right through me. He immediately turns and walks back around his car. He doesn't say anything to me and drives off.

What now? Ugh. What is with this man? And what was he doing waiting outside my apartment? Then it hits me; he's probably just checking to make sure I didn't have any issues last night. The bookstore doesn't open until nine. I pull my phone out of my bag and check the time. It's only seven-thirty. How would he even know I would be leaving? Oh, wait. I gave my detailed agenda to Detective Marshall yesterday, I just didn't realize he paid that close of attention to it.

This is nonsense. I'm not even going to worry about him today. I have to focus on the play this afternoon. We have an opener at one o'clock for those on campus then the play is open to the public tonight at seven. It's a couple hours long so I will have enough time to grab something to eat in between performances. I'm pretty sure Mark is having lunch catered, as well.

I jump in my car but first check my surroundings. I don't notice anything out of the ordinary. I head on class.

Dress rehearsal starts at ten. We will have an hour for lunch before the one o'clock show begins. Rey and I help each other with our hair and makeup. She first straightens my hair and then curls it into beach waves, which shortens it up to my collar bone. My brown hair is flowing, and my makeup has a darker, intimate look. Rey nailed my eye lashes. I'm going to have to ask for her secret.

I'm wearing my gray leg warmers with my black leotard and an oversized Midtown sweater. I walk out on stage with Rey. Carson joins us. We are all in our positions as the music starts. We listen for the music to begin and count…five, six, seven, eight.

The show ends, and we go out for drinks afterwards to celebrate. Rey and Carson ride with me while Mark, Toby and Cori all ride together. I pull up to McVey's next to Toby's car.

"Hey, Mark said drinks were on him," Toby laughs.

"Well, well, first Kat and now drinks are *on* you," Rey jokes.

"Will you stop, Rey?" I giggle back. "Mark was a perfect gentleman last night."

"That's only because I was tired. Probably not so 'perfect' tonight," Mark says as he grabs my hand. We walk inside with smiles on our faces.

It was a good night. The shows ran smoothly, and we had a large crowd. Rey's pitch on key and I didn't miss a count. If we can pull this off the rest of the weekend, we will surely get good reviews. I know it's important to Mark. It is his first show and I want him to do well. He's been a nervous wreck all week, it's nice to see him relax.

We order drinks and grab a table. The bar has a nice crowd. Music is going, and the atmosphere is upbeat. We kick back and enjoy ourselves. Laughter rattles amongst us and the drinks flow. I'm enjoying myself. I head to the bar to grab another bucket of beers. I see some of our castmates.

"Hey, Jane," I say. Jane turns around. There's no other word for Jane than the word 'stunning'. She has long, slick, straight brunette hair. Her face is sculpted with her skin flawless. She's tall and lanky. She could pass for a model if one didn't know better. She's the girl every other girl wishes they were.

"Hey, girl, great job tonight!" she exclaims.

"Oh, thanks, you too!" I say putting my hand on her arm. "We have a table over there if you want to join us!" Looking around, I don't see any other cast member.

"Actually, I'm here with someone but I'm sure he won't mind," she says.

"Who are you here with? Where is he?" I ask.

"Oh, he's right here." She touches the man standing behind her. He turns around. It's Chad. "Chad, I want you to meet someone. This is Kat, Kat this is Chad." She is proud to show him off. Who wouldn't be? I'd be walking around with him like he's a prize; 'everyone come look new toy'.

"Hi," I say innocently. He doesn't respond.

"The crew has a table over there and have asked us to join," she states. "What do you say?"

He looks at me, turns to look at the table and grins. "Sure, why not?"

"Great," I say with zero excitement in my tone as we head back to the table.

"Officer Lovely?" Rey asks surprised when we walk up to the table.

"Officer Lakes, actually, but you can call me Chad."

"Nah, I'll stick with Officer Lovely," Rey insists.

"You guys know each other?" Jane asks.

"Oh, yeah, he comes to our apartment all the time," Rey says. Her and Jane aren't the best of friends. Jane is jealous Rey got the lead vocals in the play. So, Rey enjoys being petty any chance she can get.

"Wait, what?' Jane turns and looks at Chad for confirmation.

"I've had to take these drunk girls home before. You think they would learn," he says looking at our pitcher of beer. "I sure hope you girls aren't driving."

"Uber," Rey says while burping. The table laughs.

"Anyways, that's Tobi, Cori, and Mark," she finishes going around the table.

"Chad knows Mark, too," Rey chimes in. "He was there the third time Chad came over."

"You've been there three times? How much do you girls drink?" Jane asked.

"Three times, really?" Mark asked.

Chad chimes in, "They drink a lot."

I sit down next to Mark and Chad sits across from me in the middle Jane and Rey. I try to continue my conversation with Mark. He puts his hand on my knee. It's awkward for me. All I can think about is the fact he and Jane are together right now. How long have they been dating? How come I didn't know this? Why did he kiss me and why was he waiting for me outside the apartment this morning? I kick Rey underneath the table. She can read my eyes. I know I can count on her.

"Did you just kick me?" Chad asks.

I spit out my drink. Shit. "Sorry, I was trying to get Rey's attention," I say wiping off my mouth.

Rey bursts out into laughter. "Way to go, dumbass."

"Yeah, dumbass," Chad says dryly.

I pick up my beer and continue to act normal. Rey can see that I'm shook up a bit. She reads my tone though my eyes.

"So, Chad, how long have you and Jane been dating?" Rey picks up on my hint.

"About two weeks," Jane says excitedly.

"Two weeks?" Rey asks. "Heck, he's probably been at our house more than he has yours, then!"

Jane is silent. I love Rey; she knows how to shut anyone up.

"Jane, why didn't you tell us you were dating anyone; we see you every day? Better yet, Chad, why haven't you visited her on the set?"

Jane tries to cut Chad off before he can answer, "Well, it hasn't been anything serious, so I didn't want to mention it. Plus, he's got a real big case going at work and has been putting in extra hours trying to solve it," she says while wrapping her arm around his.

Both Rey and I simultaneously spit out our drinks this time.

"What the fuck, girls?" Mark asks.

"Sorry, sorry! It's just funny to me," I say. Chad puts his hand about his eyebrows as if he's feeling a tension headache coming on.

"What's funny?" Jane asks.

"Nothing. Nothing is funny," I say.

Rey cutting me off, "So, Chad, why were you outside the apartment this morning?"

"Wait, you were outside *their* apartment?" Mark asks using his pointer finger.

Chad swallows his drink, "Well, I was outside my parents' bookstore, so yes."

Nice cover. That's what I would say, too. Although, it does make sense.

"Well, this isn't how I expected this conversation to go. Are you ready, Chad? Jane stands up.

"Yep." Chad sets his drink down, stands up and pushes his chair back under the table. "You girls," he says looking back and forth at me and Rey, "don't drive."

They start to walk away, Jane in front of Chad, and suddenly she stops and turns around. She steps up on her toes and gives Chad a kiss.

That bitch. She's doing it out of spite.

Chad succumbs to her lips and begins to kiss back.

That dick.

I can't help but stare. I'm like an eight-year-old girl watching her thirteen-year-old sister make-out with her boyfriend. This is ridiculous, I can't take my eyes off of them. I was the girl he was kissing just a few days ago. How is it her? Are we taking turns now? Who gets to kiss Chad next? Is this the adult version of spin-the-bottle? This is bullshit.

"This is bullshit," I stand up. I aggressively push my chair underneath the table and stomp off to the best of my ability, I have had a few drinks after all, but not without 'accidently' bumping my shoulder into Chad's back. It breaks up the kiss. Thank God.

"Oh, excuse us," Jane says condescendingly.

Dear self, remind self that I now hate Jane. It would be a shame if she fell off stage. I wonder if Rey can make that happen. Okay, that's awful of me. Maybe I could do something a little less tragic, like spit on her lipstick.

"Katy, you're drunk," I say aloud to myself. It was time I called Uber. Where's my phone? Wait, where's my purse? Damn it, it's at the table. How am I supposed to go back to the table when I stomped off? Well, you're going to walk your ass back there, that's how. Logical Katy hates drunk Katy. Drunk Katy hates Logical Katy.

I walk my ass back to the table where Mark is still sitting. "Are you okay? What was that about?" he asks.

"Nothing. I'm going home. I just need my purse. Rey, let's go," I demand.

"Yes, sir." She stands up, "Let's go Carson, Katy is on a rampage." Carson huffs but does what he's told. "We are better off just doing what she says."

I remain silent. She knows I'm aggravated.

"Wait, Katy, you don't need to drive," Mark says.

"Uber." I walk off waving my hand while remaining to look forward. We head outside to wait for the Uber. "I just want to go home."

"Don't let those two get the best of you," Rey says. "You know how I feel about Jane, just ignore her. Now, Chad, you guys only kissed once, that doesn't mean anything."

"Whoa, you kissed Chad?" Carson chimes in. "What about Mark?"

I ignore the question. "You're right, but it was a good kiss. And did you see those eyes of his? I'm wet just thinking about him staring me down."

"You kissed Chad?" Carson tries again for an answer.

"You'll be fine. You just need to sleep it off. We have a big day tomorrow, let's go home," Rey tries to console me as the Uber shows up.

"Am I invisible?" Carson wonders aloud.

We climb in the Uber and head home. All I can think about is how Jane was so rude. She's obviously jealous that Officer Lakes has been at our apartment.

We pull up to the apartment and scoot our way out of the backseat.

"Guys, is your door is supposed to be open?" Carson asks.

I look and see that our green downstairs door has been kicked in. Suddenly, I sober up. "Oh. My. God." I know who did this. It has to be the guy who's breaking into the bookstore. Why is he breaking into our apartment? What does he want? "I'm calling Jane. We need Chad to get here."

"Don't call Chad, call 911," Rey suggests.

"You call 911, I'm calling Jane." I start to pace back and forth. "Pick up, come on Jane, pick up. Jane! Is Chad with you? Well where did he go? Can you call him; we need him at our apartment. No, I'm not being petty, we need him. Can you help us or not?" I hang up. She really is a bitch.

I put my phone back in my purse and as I'm pacing back and forth waiting for Rey to hang up with the police, I see a man walking up to us. It takes me a moment, but I realize it's Chad.

"What are you doing here?" I ask frantically.

"I came to check on the store. What's wrong?" He notices my apartment door. "Did you do that?"

"Yes. No! Someone kicked it in. Rey is on the phone with the police now."

"Yes. Actually, Officer Lovely just walked up. I don't know his real name, I know him by Officer Lovely." Rey is drunk. He just told him his name less than an hour ago.

"Lakes! My last name is Lakes!" he snaps at her.

"Officer Asshole—I mean Lakes, is here," she tells dispatch.

"I don't have time for this. You guys stay here, I'm going upstairs," Chad tells us.

"No, Chad. What if someone is in there?" I beg of him.

"I'll be fine. Stay here and wait for the police," he brushes me off and heads up the stairs.

"My god, talk about sexual tension. That guy wants to dick you." Carson says.

I ignore him. It's more like I want him to dick me. Will you hush, Katy? You have more important things to worry about right now. Someone just broke into your apartment, I tell myself.

Within a few minutes the police show up. Chad comes back downstairs, "the place is empty. I can't tell if anything is missing. You girls will have to check it out yourselves. You will have to give a statement to the officer and he will report it back to Detective Marshall." He looks at me, "There's no way to tell if this is related to the store."

I am scared. What if it is related to the store? What if we were home and our door got kicked in? Is this person watching me or just reckless and irrelevant to the store incidents?

I give a statement to the police. Rey is in no condition to talk to any officer. Chad takes her upstairs to scope the place out, Carson follows.

I finish giving my statement and head up the stairs, myself. I look around the living room and see that nothing is out of place. I hear voices in the back bedroom. I walk down the hall to see everyone in Rey's room. "Well, is anything missing?"

"Not on my end. But you should check out your room to be sure." Rey's room looks fine and intact. I turn around and cross the hall.

My room appears to be the way I left it. I look around to double check and see that my jewelry box lid is lifted. I didn't leave that lifted, did I? I walk over to my vanity to see. I open up my necklace box, and my necklace my mom gave me when I younger, is missing. "Chad!"

Chad walks in, "What, what's wrong?"

"My necklace is gone. It was one that my mother gave me when I was little. It was a cross with a diamond in the middle of it."

"How much is it worth?" he asks.

"I don't know, not much I wouldn't think."

"You'd be surprised what crack addicts take for a hit," he says.

"So, you don't think it's related?' I ask.

"I wouldn't rule it out, but I'm thinking since you are that close to the south side, it's probably just some ghetto soul looking to buy a rock."

"You sound confident."

"As much crime as I see, you can never speculate. You take each case for what it is," Chad says. "Now, are you girls going to be okay for the night? I'll call in and ask for extra patrol in the area tonight."

"I'm here, too, we'll be fine," Carson peaks in.

"Yeah, I guess we'll be fine," I say as we walk back to the front door.

He opens the door, "Well, if you need anything, call your boyfriend." He walks out.

The hectic weekend comes to an end on after the matinee show on Sunday. I change my clothes back into my everyday wear of black yoga pants, a navy blue long tee and my black flats. I'm exhausted. I have danced for three days straight and just want to put on my sweats and lay in my bed. I walk out of the dressing room and up the stairs. I see a group of people blocking the door conversing.

"Excuse me," I say, trying to pass through. Around turns Chad, holding a bouquet of white lilies with long stems wrapped in tissue paper. I'm stopped dead in my tracks. For the first time ever, I am breathless. His eyes have made my body limp. I grab the bar leading up the steps to keep my balance. He has trimmed his beard to the precision of his jawline. He's wearing a charcoal colored sports jacket over a navy-blue V-neck tee with jeans. How am I supposed to speak when I can't even breathe? "Chad. I didn't know you were going to be here."

"Oh, yeah, hey." he responds holding out the flowers.

I smile as I reach for the bouquet. He got *me* flowers! He came to see *me*! How can someone as handsome as him bring someone like me flowers? Am I dreaming? There's a card. *For you, from Me.* It makes me smile. It sounds like his humor; dry and arrogant.

He pulls the flowers back, "Oh, I'm sorry. These are actually for Jane."

Of course, they are. How can I be so stupid? Logical Katy is hitting her forehead right now.

"Yes, of course, she'll be right up," I say. "Excuse me."

He steps to side for me to pass through, "Hey, Katy," I turn, "great job up there."

"Thanks." I smile and walk out the door.

Kathy called me wanting us to have a staff meeting tonight. It must be something important if she's calling us on a Sunday evening. It's been pretty quiet around the neighborhood since the break-in, so it might be something else other than that.

I left the auditorium, grabbed a sandwich. I text Rey to tell her I was going to a meeting, she responded telling me she was headed to the gym. I put my phone in my back pocket and walked into work. Andrea and Samantha are standing behind the counter talking to Kathy. Kathy looks nice today. She's wearing a blue blouse tucked into her black pencil skirt. I wonder what that's about. She's usually a kimono gal.

"With everything that's been going on, we feel this is the best option. So, from this point on you will report to him or Caleb. Understand?" Kathy says.

"Yes, ma'am. Not a problem," Samantha replies while both turn to look at me.

"Katy, glad you're here. I need to talk to you," Kathy says.

"Sorry, I'm late. Am I in trouble? I ask. It wouldn't surprise me if I am. It seems like lately I've done nothing but get into trouble. My mom yelled at me the yesterday for not telling her about the break-in, myself. I wasn't going to tell her, but Rey let it 'slip' she claims. I just didn't want to worry her.

"No," Kathy replies.

The front door chimes. Here comes Chad walking in. I instantly roll my eyes. Once again, this man leaves me gasping for air. If only he wasn't an arrogant, egotistical asshole maybe I would be attracted to him more than just a physical attraction.

"What are you doing here?" I ask.

"I'm your new boss."

Chapter 7

"What?" I look to Kathy for confirmation.

"We have decided to add security to the bookstore. My son, Caleb, owns a security company and he has offered to keep an eye on the store. Someone will be here when we open to when we close. They will look like customers throughout the day. During the slow periods, they will take their lunches. They understand that if someone comes in, they must stop what they're doing and come back out onto the floor. If there are any problems, all my sons have worked at the bookstore and know all the procedures. From now on, you will report to them. If these break-ins are in relation to me, I need to stay away from the store. I won't be around for a while. Do you understand?"

"Yes," all three of us girls say simultaneously. "Does this start today?" I ask looking around for someone else who could possibly be her son.

"Yes. Caleb is here and will help Andrea close."

"Caleb? Then what is Chad doing here?" I ask confused.

"Caleb has a business to run, as well. Chad is taking off for a while to help us out," Kathy confirms.

Well, isn't this just great. Now, I have to deal with him at work, not only just working with him, but he's now my boss. I like coming here. I get to read books in a peaceful environment, sip my latte's, and deal with mature patrons.

It's not like other retail jobs, this one is pleasant. Well, it *was*.

Caleb comes walking out from behind an aisle. He's just as breathtaking as Chad. He's older with salt and pepper hair with a clean-shaven face. He has broad shoulders. I could see myself wrapped up in his arms and feel safe. Not only is he wearing a wedding ring, he's wearing a blazer as well. I bet Kathy makes them all wear blazers to Sunday dinner. I smile. That makes me laugh at myself.

"Girls, this is Caleb, he's my middle son, he owns Lakes Security," Kathy says with a smile on her face. Middle son? I didn't know Chad had two brothers.

"Samantha, Andrea, this is Chad. He's my youngest son. He's a police officer here in town; you're in good hands," Kathy says while her face falls flat.

I wonder what her husband does for a living. Two of her sons are in the field of protection. I speculate her husband is in the field of law, as well.

"Hi, Chad. It's nice to meet you." By the look on Samantha's face, she is mesmerized by his stunning good looks as well. Andrea can't seem to take her eyes off Caleb.

"Okay, well, now that's over, I'm going home." She picks up her Louis Vuitton bag and puts on her Gucci sunglasses. I didn't realize selling books made such a profit. She heads to the back of the shop and walks out.

Samantha and I are still in a daze looking at Chad. I can't get enough of his eyes. He's so busy catching a criminal, he doesn't realize what his eyes are doing to me is criminal.

He turns to look at us and catches us staring at him. I look at Samantha and give a sly wink. I know what she's thinking. She's thinking what I'm thinking; how I'd like to lick chocolate syrup off his chest.

"Is that it?" Samantha asks looking at Caleb.

"Yes, for now. You are free to go, Samantha, is it?" Caleb asks.

"You can call me Sam."

"Okay. I've met Andrea, but you are?" he looks at me with those intense blue eyes.

Does Kathy have blue eyes? If she does, they don't compare two these two men's eyes. "I'm Katy, but you can call me Kat."

"Like a kitty cat?" Caleb and Chad must think alike. That's annoying.

"Yes, like a kitty cat," Chad chimes in laughing.

I can't believe he's my boss now. This is aggravating. Wait until I tell Rey. She will be down here all the time knowing there's a chance Jane could walk in at any moment. Rey is so hung up on being catty with her. She has talked about Jane all morning on Saturday; before the play, during the play, all day today.

"Alright, well, I've had all of the fun I can take here today. I'm going home." I pick up my bag from the countertop and start to leave.

"Goodbye, Kitty Cat."

"Goodbye, Chad." I walk out. I know he's just pestering but I'm over it. I just can't read the man. One minute we're kissing, the next he's kissing Jane. One minute he's checking in on me, the next he's bringing flowers to someone else. He's confusing, baffling, mystifying, ugh, I need to relax. It's been a rough weekend.

I walk upstairs to find my apartment quiet, "Rey? You home?" I check her bedroom and the bathroom; the rooms are vacant. This gives me an opportunity to take a nap peacefully. I kick off my shoes and pull back my covers. I slide into bed and I'm out.

"Don't worry, sweetie, we'll get you some clothes. How about you and I spend the rest of the day shopping? How does that sound?" Carol tries to cheer me up.

I nod my head, but I can't smile. The tears are flowing too hard. Carol said Daddy is going to be busy for a while and that I'm going to be staying there with her. I get to sleep in a real bed, which is nice, but I sure do miss Daddy.

Carol and I go to town and go shopping. Carol likes jewelry. She wears a lot of it. She says accessories are an exclamation point to your outfit. I just learned about exclamation points in school. I can't wait for school to start again. I miss my friends.

Carol got me a necklace. It's pretty. It's go a diamond in it. I've had a diamond before. She said I should wear it all the time and when I'm having a bad day, I just rub it and it will make me feel better. She picks out some outfits for me and buys me a new pair of tennis shoes. They light up when I jump. They make me smile. I jump a lot in the store. My smile gets bigger.

Carol likes to cut hair. She takes me to a haircutting place. I've never been to one of these before. She washes my hair and massages my head. It feels good. She says she's trimming the edges, whatever that means, and that she likes my hair. I like her hair, too. She's curly like me.

She said soon that we will go see the judge and she can be my new Mommy. My mommy might be sad. I do like Carol. She tucks me in at night. The blankets smell good. She said the judge has a gravel. I guess he likes rocks. But she said the gravel goes boom. Boom.

I wake up sweating. I hear a banging on the door. I bet Rey forgot her keys. I throw the blankets off of me and head down the hallway.

"Hang on, I'm coming," I yell. As I open the door, "Did you forget your ke--." I'm stopped dead in my tracks. "Mark. What are you doing here?"

"You ok? You look flushed?" Mark says.

"Oh," I feel the heat radiating off my face. I step back to let Mark inside. "Yeah, I just woke up."

"You sure?" he questions.

"Yeah, yeah I'm fine. What's going on? Everything okay?" I asked surprised to see him on the other side of the door.

"Well, I came to check on you. You left in a hurry after the play."

"Oh, sorry. I had a meeting at the bookstore, I had to bail quickly."

"Ah. I just wanted to make sure I didn't do anything to upset you."

"Why would I be upset?" I'm actually more annoyed than upset.

"I don't know, just paranoid I guess." He sits down on the couch.

Why is he sitting on the couch? I didn't tell him to have a seat. This is irritating. I don't want company right now, I want to go back to sleep.

"You couldn't just text me?" Why am I so crabby? Because I've had a long weekend, that's why.

"I guess I could have, but I wanted to see you, too."

"Oh." I say unimpressed.

"Are you sure you're ok?" he double-checks.

"Yeah," I say rubbing my temples, "I'm fine. I'm just exhausted from the weekend."

"Well, I'll let you go back to bed then." He stands up. He sounds frustrated. I'm not trying to be rude, I'm just tired.

"Okay," I stand up after him. I should invite him to stay. It's not his fault I'm cranky. Maybe tomorrow I'll feel better, I ask him then.

"Well, you have a good night," he says.

I open the door and he leans in for a kiss. I hear the downstairs door close. I quickly turn my head and he kisses my cheek. He turns around to see who's coming up the stairs.

"Sorry, I didn't mean to interrupt anything. I'll wait outside," Chad says.

Chad? Why is Chad here? I peak my head outside the door and he's dressed in his police uniform.

"Chad? What's going on?" I ask surprised to see him. He doesn't move from the downstairs door.

"I'll wait," he replies.

"No, it's fine, Mark was just leaving."

Mark turns and looks at me. "You sure you don't want me to stay?"

"No, I'll be fine. Plus, it's probably confidential information regarding the case," I say trying to get rid of him.

"Alright, I'll text you tomorrow." He leans in for another kiss and this time I bow my head and he kisses my forehead.

"Alright, I'll see ya."

He heads down the stairs while Chad is still standing at the bottom. Chad opens the door for him as if he's glad to see him go. I smile at his gesture. The door closes, and Chad heads up the stairs.

"What's up? I thought you were taking a leave of absence? Is everything okay? Did something happen at the bookstore again?" I ask concerned.

"Let's go inside," he suggests.

We walk inside and sit on the couch. I slouch into the cushions while he sits straight up. It must be serious.

"Okay, you're making me nervous," I say. I sit up and cross my legs.

He looks so attractive in his uniform. All I can think about right now is how this would be one awesome porno. I can see myself ripping off his uniform and him handcuffing me to my metal post bed. I'm turned on just thinking about it. I can feel my face turning red. Okay, time to knock it off. Concentrate.

"I ended things with Jane."

"Oh? Why?" Why would he tell me this?

"This is going to be difficult to say," he pauses, "I can't stop thinking about you."

"What?" I say without thinking.

"I know, I shouldn't have come here. I know you have a boyfriend, but I couldn't take it any longer."

"What?" I say again without thinking. What is happening right now?

"Can you say something else?"

"What do you want me to say? I'm a little taken back at the moment." I'm not lying. Where did this come from? He's always so conceited around me. I pause, "What brought this on?"

"This is really hard for me to say. I'm not the kind of person that says things like this. So, bear with me." He takes a breath, "Ever since that first time you threw up on me a few weeks ago, I've constantly been thinking about how someone so innocent looking could be such a destruction to society?"

"Excuse me?" I say. What the hell is he talking about? This is the worst pick-up line I've ever heard.

"I just don't understand how someone like you could keep my mind so occupied?" he stumbles over his words.

"Wow. Someone like me?"

"That sounded bad. What I mean is," he pauses, "I don't know what I'm trying to say. I just know that every time I see you, I stop breathing."

Is this real life? Is this really happening to me? He goes breathless over me? How is that even possible? "I don't know what to say."

"Well, that makes two of us," he says.

"I didn't realize this was part of your job description," I try to joke.

He smiles. "I guess what I'm trying to say is do you want to go grab some dinner?'

"Aren't you on the job?" I look at this uniform.

He looks down and chuckles, "Right. I guess I am. Okay, I work Monday and Tuesday, then I start my leave of absence. So, how about Wednesday then?"

"Wednesday night? I work until seven."

"How about I pick you up at seven o'three? he asks.

"Okay. Do you know where I live?" I say jokingly.

"Smartass." Before I can reply to his comment, dispatch comes over the radio, "We've got a 10-53 at 3839 Hillcrest Drive, 10-53 at 3839 Hillcrest Drive."

"That's me. I have to go." He stands up. "I apparently have a job to do." He walks to the door as I am still dumbfounded by this news and can't move from the couch.

"Oh, Chad?" He turns back to look at me, "I don't have a boyfriend."

"Good to know."

He walks out the door. What just happened? He was right; how could someone like me occupy his mind? Someone who is as good looking as he is could have anyone he wanted. Why hasn't someone snatched him up, yet? I can't wait to tell Rey about this.

Wait, where is Rey? I look at the clock and realize it's ten o'clock. She must be staying with Carson. I grab a drink of water and head back to bed.

Before I know it, it's noon on Wednesday. I didn't feel like going to class today, so I skipped. I jump in the shower, I don't put on any makeup yet, and run downstairs to grab me some lunch. I sit by myself next to the window and watch the people walk up and down the strip. Many are swinging their shopping bags and laughing amongst themselves. It appears as if everyone is smiling today, myself included. I don't have anything to do today, besides go with Officer Lakes this evening; which is the reason why I'm smiling. Kathy called me and said they had a water issue at the bookstore, so it isn't open today; otherwise I'd grab me some coffee. I guess I'll just drink my sweet tea instead.

I haven't spoken to Chad since Sunday night. I hope we are still on for tonight. I plan on being ready at seven o'three just to be sure.

I text my mom to check in with her. She says she's doing fine, busy with customers hair. I text Rey but no response yet; she must be in class, still. Or making out with Carson. I swear, she acts like she's still a teenager. We're both are twenty-two, about to be twenty-three. I love her to death, though. Mark text me asking if we could get together tonight. I told him I was busy. What's with the sudden mass of infatuation with me? I must be ovulating.

I go back upstairs to pick out an outfit. Ugh, scratch that. I go into Rey's closet and pick out a navy, blue quarter length cardigan with a floral cami. I put on some skinny jeans and steal a pair of her tan booties. Thank goodness for her obsession with clothes. I have plenty of accessories that she borrows from me, so we call it even. I wear some blue bangles around my wrist and matching blue earrings. My ears have double holes, but I rarely wear the second set. Tonight, I decide to put my diamond studs in. They will bring out my eyes, as my mom would say.

I finish my makeup just in time to hear a knock on the door. "I'm coming!" I yell. I hustle to the door to open it. There Chad stands. My heart skips a beat.

He's wearing a button-down, navy shirt with dark jeans and dark brown boots. The somber colors look stimulating on him. He has his short hair fixed with gel and his beard, once again, in precision with his jawline. I really want to nibble on his cheeks. Would it be inappropriate to touch his face, right now? Keep your hands down, Kat. Better yet, don't bite him. Have a little bit of self-control, damn girl.

"Hi," he says.

"Hi."

"Are you ready to go?"

"Yes, just let me grab my bag." I run back to my bedroom to grab my crossbody purse. It's white with pastel flowers. It's very 'springy' as one might say. I throw it over my neck and grab my keys.

He walks me to his black Lincoln MKZ and opens the back-passenger door for me.

I laugh. "Very funny."

"What? I'm serious," he says in his 'police' tone.

"You're kidding, right?" I ask jokingly but I'm honestly not sure if he *is* joking. I'm not used to this dry sense of humor.

He pauses, "yes, of course." He closes the door and opens the front passenger door. "You behave yourself or you *will* ride in the back seat on the way home." He winks at me. My panties are now wet.

"Where are we going?" I ask while driving down the strip.

"I made reservations at Agostino's downtown," he says.

Agostino's Restaurant and Wine Bar is one of the best five-star restaurants in Middletown. I've never been there. I rarely even go downtown. Mainly because everything down there is so expensive and I'm just a poor gal. Also, because everything I could possibly need is on the street where I live.

The car ride is a little awkward. He turns on some of today's hits on his satellite radio. It's a little awkward listening to a song that is telling me to 'back that ass up'. I turn to look at Chad and his face is stone. I wonder if he's nervous. Should I sing for him? Listening to me sing some Juvenile should lighten any mood.

I choose to save myself from the humility even though a part of my wants to 'back my ass up' into this seat. How can he not be grooving even a little bit? It's taking everything I have to not tap my feet, right now.

We finally get downtown. Very few words were spoken on the way here. If this is any indication how my date is going to go, I might as well call Mark. At least he talks to me; even if it's too much.

We pull up to valet and the attendant helps me out of the car. Chad quickly walks around and takes my arm. He tips the driver and we walk in.

"We have a reservation under Lakes at seven," he says to the host.

"Yes, Mr. Lakes, we have your usual table ready for you," the host signals his arm for us to follow.

Usual table? How often does the man eat pasta with that body? If I eat even a fork spool of spaghetti my stomach swells up like a blow fish. I should have worn leggings. With my luck my button will pop off after dinner. Why did he have to pick pasta of all genre's? He's probably doing it on purpose to see if I will actually eat or I'm a crouton and cheese girl. Oh, boy, do I love pasta. I'll eat my weight in fettucine noodles. He doesn't know what he's getting himself into, here.

The restaurant is very intimate with a touch of class. Brass chandeliers hang from the tin ceiling as white cloth covers tables with leather back chairs. On the other side of the restaurant is the wine bar. It has tan natural stone covering the walls, with wooden shelves for the wine glasses. There are barrels with spouts coming out of the wall. It looks like a restaurant straight out of Tuscany. It gives me a warm homey sensation that makes me feel like this is where I need to be.

I need to be in Italy. I should make that a goal. In fact, goal set.

"Good evening, sir Lakes and ma 'dam. Shall I bring you your usual?" the waiter asks.

"Good evening, Charles. Yes, a bottle of Rose'." He looks at me, "Do you prefer chilled or room temperature?"

Charles is tall, about Chad's height. He has a dark goatee that matches his short dark hair. His eyes are bright hazel. I haven't ever seen green eyes with speckles of blue.

"Chilled would be great," I say. What kind of place is this? He's being treated like royalty right now. Am I on a date with a prince? I chuckle at myself.

Chad nods to Charles and we open up our menus. I don't even know why I'm looking at the menu, I always get chicken alfredo. I pretend to overlook the menu. Sheesh, this shit is expensive. It costs me four bucks to make this at home. This, this right here is why I don't come downtown.

Charles comes back with the ice bucket and bottle of Rose'. He pours us both a glass. "Are you ready to order, Miss?"

"Yes, I will have the chicken alfredo."

He looks at me confused. "We don't have chicken alfredo."

Damn it. This is what I get for acting like I know what I'm doing. "How does an Italian restaurant not have alfredo?" I ask with a smile on my face with underlining annoyance in my tone.

"Katy," I look at Chad, "he's kidding."

My face fizzes out the smile that it was upon. "Oh."

Both Chad and the waiter chuckle at me. Dickheads.

"I will have the steak and potato's, medium, with sautéed green beans."

Sautéed green beans at an Italian restaurant? I just want some damn bread sticks. Why can't he be simple like me? I don't know if this will work out if we have to eat green beans all the time for dinner.

"Yes, sir. I'll put those in for you." Charles turns to walk away but not without a wink at me. He either thinks he's funny or he's blatantly flirting with me in front of Chad.

"Do you come here often?" I ask knowing the answer is yes.

"About four times a week."

"Four times a week?" I'm a big fan of pasta, but four days a week of pasta? How is he so fit if he's eating noodles as a food group? It must be the green beans. How does he afford that on a cop's salary? I wonder if he's in the mob, too.

"Yes. Our Mafia meetings happen here."

Shit. Did I say that out loud? I look at him with guilty behind my eyes.

"You're going to have to learn to take a joke. My oldest brother, Charles, our waiter, owns the place with my parents."

"Wait, your brother is our waiter?"

"Well, he's not a waiter per 'say, he's just waiting on us. He knew we were coming and he's just messing with you."

"Ah. Tricky, tricky you Lakes' boys." I want to know more. "So, your family owns this *and* the bookstore?"

"Yes. My father is a judge here in Middletown and my mother helps run the restaurant with Charlie. The bookstore is hers, though. It was hers before she met my father, almost forty years ago."

"They've been married for forty years?" Chad nods his head in response as he swallows his wine. "Mom was left the bookstore when my grandfather died just a few years ago. My grandpa was a writer and the thought the best way to sell his books was to open a store to sell them."

"Did he sell a lot of books?" I ask.

"He sold a lot. None of them were his, but he *did* sell books," Chad laughs. He seems to be comfortable here. He's loosening up. "My mom's maiden name is Pond but she married a Lakes. So, she just kept the name 'Pond's Paperbacks'.

"That's pretty clever. Ironic, but clever," I say. Not trying to change the subject but moving forward, "So, what made you become a cop? Following the law in your father's footsteps?"

"Actually, no. My parents are quite upset that I didn't go to law school. Both of my brothers' have made something of themselves. Charles owns this place but is also a financial advisor. Caleb started his own security company and I'm a blue-collar worker with shitty hours. Frankly, I chose to be a cop just to piss off my mother."

"That's terrible!" I gasp.

"No, it's not. If you knew my mother, you would understand. She's a control freak. She can't stand that she has no control over what happens when I'm out in the field."

"I do know your mother; I work for her."

"No, you work for me."

I roll my eyes. How am I supposed to get any work done with him breathing down my neck? It's taking everything I have not to jump over this table and sexually abuse him.

"I really would like to go to law school. I figured I would do this for a few more years, take what money I do make and invest it. Then by the time I decide to go back, I will have the money to pay for it myself. I don't want my parents paying for it just in case I decide it's not for me. Then they won't be out that much cash. I would never hear the end of it."

"Are you wanting to be a judge, too?" I ask out of curiosity.

"Maybe someday. With being an officer, I have learned the ropes. I've started to learn how criminals think. I would love to incriminate some of those douchebags. But the other part of me would love to indict some of them longer than what some of them are being punished now. I'm baffled how the justice system works sometimes. Sometimes the bad guy gets zero punishment while the good guy gets a longer term. I would like to balance it out the way it should be."

"So, you have two brothers, you want to be a lawyer, let's see…. have you always lived in Middletown?" I ask.

"Yes, I grew up on the north side. Went to school at Northwest Prep School, then attended Midtown University, as well."

"Midtown? Why not Rivot?" I ask.

"Once again, mainly to piss off my mother. My mother met my father at Rivot. She thinks Midtown is full of nothing about people who don't want to branch out and succeed."

"That's kind of rude," I say responding to his statement.

"Yeah, that's my mother. She is set in her ways." He takes a drink of his Rose' and asks, "So, what about you? Where did you grow up?" he asks out of curiosity.

"Well, I grew up in Middletown as well," I respond.

"Really, you're a townie, too? Where did you attend prep school?"

"I don't know if I would call it 'prep school', it's just a high school to me. And I grew up on the south side."

"Oh. I see." He acts disappointed, but we are interrupted by Charles bringing our food.

"Does everything look okay for you two?"

"Yes, thank you," I say. I pick up my fork to take my first bite while Chad is cutting up his steak.

So, finish. You grew up close to where you live now?" he asks.

"Yes. My mom lives just a few miles away."

"What does she do?"

"She is a beautician at Hair Hut over on Grand Avenue."

"I know right where that is." Of course, he does, why did I find it necessary to name the street? He works those streets five nights a week. Oh well, he's just going to have to get used to my blatant ignorance of obvious entities.

"How's your food?" I try to change the subject.

"I'm enjoying the food. And the conversation. It's nice to talk to someone that actually converses back with intelligence and doesn't get on my nerves, like Mark does.

"Do people just ignore you when you talk to them, or something?" I ask with smirk on my face.

"You seem to ignore me quite a bit."

I smile. "Yes, yes I do."

"Brat."

"Did you just call me a brat?" I laugh.

"Aren't you, though?"

"Not me," I say with a wink.

We continue to laugh throughout the evening. He tells me stories of the citizens he's run across while on duty. I laugh until I'm almost in tears. I wipe the corner of my eyes trying to fix my mascara. He's laughing with his smile peeking through. My heart flutters with happiness and the fun I'm having.

He's incredibly intriguing when he's in his element. He's quite intelligent, well spoken, serious when he needs to be and playful when his guard is down.

We leave the restaurant. It's a nice night with a little bit of a breeze. We head back to the southside. The bars are hoping in the neighborhood and the strip is crowded with regulars. He walks me to my downstairs door.

"Would you like to come up? I don't have a tv, but we can continue our talk if you want?" I ask hoping for our night to continue.

Suddenly I see Carson hustling up to me. "Kat!" He's seems frantic.

"Hey, Carson. What's wrong?" I ask nervously. I hope he's okay. He must be stopping me to let him upstairs before I lock the door behind me.

"Is Rey home?" he asks me.

"I don't know. I haven't talked to her today, in a few days actually but we've been out. I thought she was with you."

"I haven't heard from her in three days."

Chapter 8

"I'm nervous. Today is my first day at my new school. I don't know anybody. I miss my old friends. Mommy says I'll make new friends. She says I have to be brave. There's lot of people in my class. Mrs. Barlot is nice. She's got long brown hair and wears glasses. She's got a big belly. She's going to have a baby.

I sit down at my desk. I put my notepad and folders in my desk. Oops, I dropped my pencil.

"Here." A blonde girl picks it up and reaches out her hand to give it to me.

"Thank you," I reply to her. She seems nice.

"My name is Audrey," she whispers.

"I'm Katy."

The teacher brings me over some books and tells me we'll be going to lunch soon. I brought my lunch today. Mommy got me a new lunchbox with a cat on it. The cat has dark hair. Mommy said it reminded her of me. I got a pretty backpack, too. I've never had a backpack before. All of my pencils are sharpened, and my shoes are squeaky clean. Mommy got me new shorts and a pretty, pink shirt. My hair is down around my face with a bow holding back my bangs.

We line up to go to lunch. Audrey lines up behind me.

"Do you want to sit by me at lunch?" Audrey asks.

I smile. "I'd like that."

We play tag at recess. She runs fast. She told me her baby sister calls her 'Rey' because she can't say Audrey. She said the rest of her family now calls her that, too. She said I could call her Rey, too. I told her she could call me Kat, like Mommy does. And if she can't remember my name that she can look at my lunchbox. She said her birthday is on Saturday and wants me to come to her birthday party. I told her I would ask Mommy. I've never been skating before, I bet it's fun!

"Kat, will you be my best friend?"

"Yes!"

"Kat!" Carson is snapping his fingers in front of me.

I must have dazed out. "Rey; where is she?" I say rhetorically with terror in my voice.

I open the outside door and run up the stairs. I open the interior door and start to look for her. "Rey! Rey! Are you home?"

I check room after room and nothing has been touched. I go into her bedroom to see if there is anything unusual looking in her room. Her bed is still made. Her closet doors are still closed. Her shoes are still in place next to her dresser. Her phone charger is still next to her bed.

Where is she? Three days of no Rey. I grab my phone out of my purse to try to call her again. It goes straight to voicemail. "Shit." I say aloud.

The guy's come running up the stairs. Chad is on the phone.

"Yes, its been seventy-two hours since anyone has heard from her. One, zero, zero, four south Roman street, apartment A. We are upstairs. I'll be here waiting. Thank you." He hangs up the phone. "The police are on their way. I sent Detective Marshall a text as well. Hopefully we hear from him soon."

"Thank you," I say to Chad. "Carson, when is the last time you saw her?"

"She was supposed to stay with me Sunday after the play. She said she was going to go to the gym and was supposed to get ahold of me for dinner. I never heard from her. I thought maybe she met up with you and just forgot or something. When I didn't hear from her on Monday, either, I started getting paranoid. I've called her over and over and it goes to voicemail. I started getting worried, it's not like Rey to not talk. Then on Tuesday, I thought she was just mad and ignoring me on purpose. Now, today, I couldn't take it any longer I had to come see her and find out what is going on."

He's right. Rey can't stay mad at anyone for long. If they had gotten into an argument, she would have given in by now. She hasn't been texting me, calling me or even following my footsteps around the apartment. I need to call her father. Maybe she's with my mother. I pick up the phone and call my mom.

"Kat, what's wrong?" She knows I don't call this late unless something is wrong.

"Mom, have you heard from Rey?" I ask in a hurry.

"Rey? No, dear. Why? What's wrong?"

"Mom, she's missing. No one has seen her in almost three days."

"I'm on my way." Mom hangs up on me. I should have known she would come over. Great, nothing like Chad meeting my mother on the first date.

I send out a mass text message to our mutual friends; Mark, Cori, Jane and everyone else from the drama department. Maybe one of them have seen or heard from her. Only one can hope.

Where could she be? Why isn't her phone on? She would text me if something was wrong. This is so unlike her. Even is she just needed a few days of space, she would let me know. Something's not right.

How has my world turned into havoc over the last few weeks? What have I done to the universe for my world to be shaken up? Why is it being taken out on my best friend? So many questions and none of them have answers.

Why Rey? Maybe she's with her dad. She doesn't get good signal at his house, maybe that's where she is.

I pick up my phone and call her father. He's not answering. Shit. My phone is suddenly getting text message after text message with friends saying they haven't talked to Rey in a few days and wonder what's wrong. I don't respond so they won't worry. Maybe she's just fine, I try to tell myself.

But I know she's not. There's something sketchy here. Could this be related to the burglary from the other night? Surely not. That was just some junkie looking for valuables to pawn.

"I'm going to try to call the hospitals and see if maybe she's in one of them," Carson says.

"That's a good idea," I say. I hear footsteps coming up the stairs.

"Hey, Luke. Nice to see you," Chad shakes the officer's hand. "This is Officer Shepard. He's going to take a statement from you."

I love his professional tone. Stop it, Kat. No time to think about boys, it's time to worry about friends.

"First off, do you have a picture of your friend I can have for reference?"

"Yes, yes of course." I walk over to our bookshelf where there is a photo frame with a picture of us at Christmas dinner this past year. "Here, feel free to cut me out of the photo."

"And you are?" he asks.

"I'm Katy Cambridge, her roommate and best friend," I say.

"Miss Cambridge, when's the last time you heard from Rey?" he questions.

"It was Sunday after the play."

"Do you remember what she was wearing the last time you saw her?"

"Yes, actually I do. She was wearing her blue yoga pants with a yellow tank top. She was on her way to the gym," I say.

"Which gym?"

"The one down the road, Ramsey's on Roman."

"Do you know of any enemies Rey may have?" he asks me.

"No, none. She's liked by everyone."

"Tell him about Friday night," Chad chimes in.

"What was Friday night," the officer asks.

"Oh, about the break-in?"

"Break-in?" he asks.

"Yes, someone kicked down our door. The only thing missing was a necklace of mine, so we didn't feel it was important enough to call the police," I say regretting my decision.

"Ok, well next time, call and make a statement, will you?" he asks, and I nod. "What was her schedule on Sunday, do you know?"

"She doesn't work, we had our play then she just said she was going to the gym, and I thought she stayed with Carson. I just assumed she was with him," I say with my arm pointing to Carson.

Officer Shepard turns to look at Carson, "Are you Carson?"

"Yes," Carson replies.

"Who are you to Rey?" Luke asks.

"I'm her boyfriend, I guess you could say."

"Ok, I have a few questions for you as well. Let's walk over here for some privacy." They walk into the kitchen and talk low-key.

I stand there in terror looking at Chad. His eyes soften. He can tell I'm worried. He places his hand on my shoulder to comfort me, it's nice to feel the warmth and sincerity of someone.

I hear more footsteps coming up the wooden staircase. "Kat? Kat are you up here?" I'm instantly at ease. The sound of my mom's voice soothes my nerves.

"Mom, we're in here," I say in reference to the living room.

She walks in wearing her curly hair back in a low ponytail. She must have been in bed because she's wearing yoga pants and an over size Midtown University hoodie.

"What's going on? Where's Rey? Has anyone heard anything?" she asks feverishly.

"No, nothing yet. Officer Shepard is taking statements now. When's the last time you talked to her?"

"Sunday evening after they play. I told her she did a great job but then I left. Have you contacted her father?" Mom asks me.

"I tried calling him, but no answer."

"Well, I'll keep trying to call him. What else can I do?" Mom seems hellbent on helping. This is what I love about her, she wants to help in any way she can.

"No, Mom, you need to go home. You didn't to come over here; it's late. You don't need to drive yourself crazy over this. I'm sure we won't know anything until the detectives come in tomorrow morning."

"She's right. There's not much that can be done tonight," Chad brings himself into our conversation.

"I'm sorry, who's this?" Mom asks me.

"Mom, this is Chad, he's an off-duty officer. He's here to help," I say trying to avoid saying he was my date.

"That, and I'm also her date for tonight."

Welp, there goes that idea. Thanks, Chad.

"Date! Why didn't you tell me you had a date?" Mom gives me 'the look'. The look that only *I* would understand. The 'I'm going to get you' look.

"Well, it just kind of happened." I lied. I've known for three days about this date. But, he's been in my life for only a few weeks now. It's only until today he might be something more than just a crush for me. I did have a great time. He relaxed tonight and showed his personality. He's actually quite funny. And his laugh, fills my heart with excitement.

"Uh, huh." I have a feeling we are going to continue this conversation later. Are you sure you don't need anything, sweetie? Are you hungry? No, of course not you just ate. What about something to drink? I can get you some water."

"Mom, calm down. I'm fine. We're all fine. We just want to find Rey."

"There's no leads?" she asks.

"None, it's just becoming a dangerous neighborhood. Between the robbery next door and then us, I feel like I need to move."

I hadn't ever thought of that. That just rolled off my tongue. Maybe I really should move. I bet after this, Rey will be one board. Where is she? She has to be okay, it's Rey. She would fight hard to stay alive.

Thought of her being is dead is enough to make me sick. I can feel it coming on.

"Katy? Oh no, there's that look again," Chad said nervously.

"What look?" my mom asks.

"Get out of the way," Chad grabs Mom's arm as I hustle to the wooden steps out the front door. I spew everywhere. "I told you," he said looking at my mom.

"What the hell was that, Kat? Are you ok?" Mom asks surprised.

"Yeah," I wipe off my mouth with my hands, "I'm ok. Just the idea of something happening to Rey got to me." I walk back through the living room to the kitchen. I walk over to the sink to wash my hands and clean my face off.

"Gosh, Kat, are you ok?" Carson asks.

"Yeah. How's it going in here?" I ask to get the focus off of me.

"We are just finishing up. I have everything I need. I'll get started on this report and have it ready for Detective Marshall when he walks in the morning. Don't worry, we'll find her." Officer Shepard seems confident.

Me, not so much. Officer Shepard heads to the door to leave. "What the hell is that?"

"Katy. That's what *that* is," Chad laughs.

"Here, I'll clean it up." Curly Carol says.

My mom hustles to the kitchen to grab some cleaner and a rag. Officer Shepard is careful to step over the vomit. He turns and gives a Chad 'What the hell' look. Chad laughs aloud.

"See ya, man. I'll be in contact with you tomorrow." Chad shakes Luke's hand before he steps down the stairs. Mom makes her way through to clean up my mess. She's the best.

"I should be heading out, too," Carson states. "Katy, let me know once you hear something. He has my number, too, if I hear anything, I'll give you a call." He leans in and gives me a hug.

"I will. You be careful going home tonight. I'll talk to you tomorrow."

Carson shakes Chad's hand and heads out the door.

"Honey, are you sure there's nothing else you need?" Mom says putting my hair behind my ear.

"No, Mom, I'm really fine. I'm just a little distraught."

"Do you want me to stay?" Mom asks.

"Mom!" I say trying to get her to understand. "I'll lock up when everyone leaves. I'll be okay."

"Ok, if you insist. You call me if you need anything. I'm serious, Katy."

"I will, Mom. I promise."

"Okay," she leans in for a kiss on my cheek, "I'll talk to you tomorrow. Chad it was nice to meet you. You take care of her if she needs anything, understand?"

"Yes, ma'am; if she will let me. She's a feisty one," Chad says playfully.

"That's my girl. Goodnight, you two." Mom leaves and closes the door behind her.

I look at Chad, "Well, this isn't how I expected this night to go."

"Are you sure you don't need anything?"

"Why does everyone keep asking me that? It's not me anyone should be worried about. Rey is out there, somewhere, probably terrified. Who knows the last time she ate? The last time she slept?"

"You're right, but let's try to be positive. Maybe she is with her father. Maybe she just needed some time away. Don't you guys have finals coming up? With the stress of the play and finals, maybe she just needed some time to relax."

Chad seems to be optimistic. He does deal with this kind of thing on a daily basis. Maybe I should trust him?

"You need to get some rest." Chad walks over to me, puts his arms around me for a hug. I feel safe in his arms. I needed this hug more than I realized.

I release my built-up tension with a breath I didn't realize I was holding. I relax in the comfort of his arms. I look up at him, he's much taller than me. He leans his head down and kisses my forehead. My soul drops to my feet and I feel secure. My infatuation is growing stronger, quickly.

"Are you sure you're going to be okay? I will call and have extra patrol. I will feel much better knowing you are safe." He lets loose of my body and slides is hand into mine. We stand there, hand in hand, looking into each other's eyes. I can't hold back.

"Will you stay with me?" I blurt out.

"You're not going to puke on me, are you?"

We both crawl into bed. He moves Miss Katy out of the way and onto my vanity.

"She's ferocious," he says.

"Very."

I'm wearing a cami and a pair of athletic shorts. I went across the hall to Rey's room and grabbed a pair of Carson's shorts. They seem to be similar in size. I had brushed my teeth, so Chad didn't have to smell the raunchy dragon breath coming from my mouth.

I'm quite nervous. I like Mark, but not in a way that even comes close to the feelings I'm beginning to develop with Chad. I even put breath mints in my nightstand just to prepare for the morning breath I will have. I'm not sure why I care so much about what he thinks of me. If he had dragon breath, I wouldn't mind. I would still stick my tongue down his throat.

Gosh, Kat, you're such a lady. Who am I kidding? At this moment, I would do just about anything for him to kiss me. I can only imagine what he's thinking; 'please don't let her turn around, if I smell her puke, I'm going to puke.' Do I really even care? He should like me regardless of the odor coming from inside me trying to exhale. Well, I say that but I'm still going to try my best not to breathe on him.

I'm being ridiculous. I roll over to look at his face. He's on his side looking back at me. "Thank you for staying,' I say.

"I'm glad you asked. I would prefer to stay to know you're safe. What if the thief cam back and you were here alone?"

I hadn't thought of that. What if he *did* come back? What would I do, honestly? I would surrender. Here take my four dollars in my wallet. I have a coupon card from McAlister's, you can have my free tea. I chuckle to myself.

"What's so funny?" Chad asks.

"Nothing, I'm just thinking."

"Care to share?"

"It's nothing really, just making a joke in my head."

"It is about me?" he asks.

"No, it's about me if I get robbed. I wouldn't know what to do."

"And you're laughing about that?" he asks.

"You would just have to be inside my head to understand." I have another place I would like him to be inside of.

Damn it, Katy. Get your mind out of the gutter and focus. How am I supposed to focus? I only have the sexiest man I have ever seen laying in bed next to me.

He caresses my arm with his fingertips. I'm trying to control my composure, but my vagina isn't cooperating. I get squirmy. I can't focus. Try harder, Kat. Try. Harder. Is he hard? How is he keeping his shit together? I'm jealous of his maturity. Here I am, all hot and bothered just by him rubbing my arm. Imagine if he touched me anywhere else, I would be pouring in my panties.

What is wrong with me? Why am I so out of mind? It's him. He makes me crazy. He makes me mad. He's still the most arrogant man I've ever met. But looking into his eyes, I see something calm. I see compassion, I see love. I see how he has a heart and can put it to good use.

"You look like you're in deep thought," he notices.

I'm wishing something was deep. "I'm sorry, my mind is in a million different places right now." No, it's not. It's on one thing and one thing only. I'm losing control here.

"Let's continue our conversation from earlier," he suggests, "maybe it will help you get your mind off things."

Yes, please do. "Okay, what do you want to know?"

"Well, for starters, what are you going to school for? I had never asked you."

"I want to be a dancer, full time. But I realize it's only for a limited time. So, I'm getting a degree in political science."

"Really? Are you going to attend law school?"

"I've definitely thought about law school, but not sure I have the drive right now. I'm thinking that while I'm young I should pursue dance and then possibly go to law school later. Unless something better comes along. You know, like working at the bookstore for the rest of my life."

"Ha, very funny."

"I'm going to need a raise," I say jokingly.

"Me too. My mother isn't even paying me. I'm doing this out of the generosity of my heart. But I honestly don't mind. Whatever keeps my family safe, I'm willing to do."

Now, that's a man. A man who sacrifices for his family. That's even more of a turn on. I really need to cool my jets. You can do this. You can pull yourself together. It's just a normal conversation; you do this every day. You can talk to him, just stop thinking and start speaking.

"Well, I met your mom tonight? What about your father?" he asks.

I knew this was coming. This is the question I want to avoid in all aspects of life. What do I tell him? That my dad was a gambler and sacrificed his daughter for a bet he owed. That's what happened. He left me because he couldn't pay a debt. How do I explain that to someone?

"I don't have a father. He abandoned me when I was eight. My birth mother left me when I was even younger. I don't remember much of her. But my mother now, adopted me. She *is* my mother. I don't like to talk about it."

"I'm sorry, I didn't mean to pry. I had no idea." Chad didn't know, how could he possibly? This is a trigger that sends me back to a time I would prefer to forget.

I start to yawn, I'm getting comfortable. I've brought the blankets up to my shoulders.

"Are you cold?" Chad asks.

"No, just getting sleepy."

"I am, too." He lays on his back and puts his arm around me as I curl up on his chest.

Is this really happening? I've been waiting for this moment and all I can do is think too much. What if I drool on his chest? My dragon breath is going to leak onto his chest. Mental note; use the sheet to wipe it off. Don't go to sleep before him. I need to let him get comfortable with me and then I can get comfortable with him.

That plan isn't working. I'm already comfortable. His arm wrapped around me gives me peace. It gives me hope that Rey is okay. It gives me a chance to feel free and not so wound-up all of the time.

My mind starts to clear, I'm beginning to doze off.

Chapter 9

It's almost Christmas. My classroom is covered in candy cane's and Christmas trees. Mrs. Barlot has lights on her tree. They twinkle. It's pretty. Mrs. Barlot says we get to have a party this afternoon. There's going to be cupcakes and candy. We get to play games. I'm excited. I like games. My mom will play games with me. She likes tic-tac-toe. I'm really good at the game. I win every time!

Since I got a perfect score on my spelling test, Mrs. Barlot says I get to be first in line to go to the gym to play and I get to pick the game we play. I also get a treat out of the treasure box. I have a treasure box. I keep pictures of me and Daddy in it. I also keep the jewelry Mommy got me, in it. It's sitting on my dresser. I have a snow globe on my dresser, too. It's got a ballerina dancing in the snow.

I'm a dancer now. My mom pays for me to take classes. She says I'm good at it. I twirl, and leap and I can do the splits now. Mommy wants me to do competitions. Rey does competitions. Rey's a dancer, too. We're in the same class, also. Rey is really good at dancing.

We line up for gym time. I stand proudly at the beginning of the line. This is my line. I'm in charge. Rey is standing behind me. She keeps whispering in my ear. She says I *should be wearing a conductor's hat and should toot my horn. I giggle. She makes me giggle a lot.*

We walk down the hall into the gym. I have decided we should play Red Rover. Rey stands next to me hand in hand and we won't let anyone break us apart. I think we are the strongest in the class. Red Rover, Red Rover, send Christy right over. Christy runs hard, but not hard enough! Rey and I give each other a high five! We have our own special hand shake. No one knows it but us.

Red Rover, Red Rover send Katy right over! I run really hard to break through the boys' arms. I can do it, I can do it! Run, run, run, bam!

I sit straight up. What was that? I look over to Chad but he's not there. Where did he go? Did he leave? Is someone here? I slowly creep out of bed. I look to see if anyone is in the bathroom, but the light is on. I tip-toe down the hallway. I hear movement. I flip on the hallway light.

"Jesus Christ," Chad jumps, "you scared the shit out of me."

"You! Me! I heard a noise and you weren't in bed. I didn't know where you went or who was here."

"Sorry, I was trying to get something to drink but my cup hit the floor. I didn't mean to wake you," he apologizes.

"You're fine, it just scared me." I flip on the kitchen light and head over to the cupboard. I grab me a cup and open the fridge. I pour a glass of tea and sit down on one of the barstools. "Do you really think Rey is okay?"

"I do. I think she probably just needed a break. Sometimes I do that. I just disappear and turn off my phone. I like to isolate myself. Sometime work is just too much for me. The things I see, the words I hear, sometimes it is overwhelming. I don't blame her, really."

"It's just, she's never done this before; not without telling me. We do everything together. We go everywhere together. We have this connection and friendship some people don't ever experience. I can't imagine her just blowing me off. I just know there's something is wrong."

"Maybe so. But you have the best officers on the case. I wouldn't say that if I didn't mean it. Detective Marshall is really good at his job. He's arrogant at times, but that's because there's no one around better than him, and he knows it. His staff trusts him, and he trusts his staff. The dynamic works and they are a good team."

"What about you?" I ask.

"What about me?" Chad replies.

"Are you part of the dynamic?" I'm curious to see if he's going to brag on himself, as well.

"Fucking right, I am. He's the reason I haven't quit yet. He's taught me how to tell when people are bullshitting and when they are honest. You'd be surprised at the amount of lies I hear daily. 'He hit me first, she tried to set me on fire,' it's absurd what goes on around you."

"You mean, our neighborhood?" I ask astounded.

"This is the southside, Katy."

"Yeah, but it's a nice area. All of the shops, the people walking up and down the strip- "

"All of the projects and ghetto neighborhoods two streets over. It's nothing but drugs and mayhem down here."

"How come I didn't know this?" I ask stupefied.

"You said you grew up down here, right? You're used to it. You've learned to adapt to your surroundings."

"Wow. All this time I thought I was living in a nice suburban area next to the college. How stupid am I?

"You're not stupid, it is nice for tourist and college families. But, they only travel the strip. They don't take the side streets in the residential areas."

He's right. I guess I don't get out of my bubble much. I go to school, work, back to the apartment. I'll occasionally go to my mom's, but I'm so used to the neighborhood, I don't even pay attention. Did I grow up in the ghetto? No, surely not. Sure, a couple blocks over isn't the best part of town, but where I lived always seemed to have a happy glow to it.

"Up until this time, I never realized all of the crime this town had. Does the northside have this much crime?" I ask.

"Sure, they have crime, but it's white collar crime, not ghetto crime. Everyone up there has tampered with their funds someway or another. But nothing like the destruction of the southside. Patrol is calm there. Very rarely are there calls. Mainly because everyone on the southside doesn't have a car or they are too obliterated to get to that part of town."

"You're really making me feel safe here, Chad."

He laughs, "Sorry, that's not what I'm trying to do."

He walks around the counter and faces me. He looks into my eyes. His eyes are penetrating, I can't look anywhere else. He leans forward and puts his fingers underneath my chin. He lifts my jaw and leans in for a kiss. His lips are soft, and the magnitude of chemistry is extreme. I can barely contain my composure.

He pulls away slowly and I open my eyes, staring into his eyes makes me feel charged. I can do anything looking into his eyes. He brings a passionate sinfulness to my soul.

He grabs my hand and leads me to the bedroom. He slowly lays me on the bed as he hovers over me. He exhales on my neck and I begin to quiver. He brings his lips to my neck and works his way down to my collar bone. He places his hand on my hip and fervently glides his hand up to my chest.

I wrap my arms around his neck bringing him closer. My mouth opens wider to be able bring his soul closer to mine. I want every piece of him I can get. The passion stimulates me to produce wetness. I want him. I need him. My hands go to his waist and begin to pull his shorts down. I can't take much more.

His hand gravitates to my shorts and yanks them down. I can feel him hard against my thigh. His hand glides down and his fingers slowly enter me. I gasp. He eases in and out teasing me. I try to shift his body on top of me and he's being stubborn. He won't give.

So, he likes to be in control. Normally I would argue it with my body, but I'm in too deep to stop. My back arches to the succumbing of him. He finally gives in and lays back on top of me. He slides slowly into me. He brings my hips closer to his pelvis. He goes in deep. I start to moan, and he goes harder. He begins to pound into me as I take every inch of him. I begin to breathe heavier. He slides his dick deep and pulls out to the tip. He does this over and over as I breathe in synchronization.

I can't take much more. I wrap my legs around his waist and lift my hips. He's deeper than he was before. My muscles start to tighten around him. He hammers into me faster and harder. I can feel my blood pumping and my heart racing. I'm to the brink of exploding around him. He runs my nipples through his fingers and I am pushed over the edge. I breathe in as his penis throbs inside of me.

He moans as he pumps harder and exhales as he cums deep inside of me. His body drops on to mine as I feel his heavy breathing tickle my neck. He nibbles on my ear and I giggle. Every bit of him inside of me falls out.

I throw my hand to my forehead as I try to catch my breath. He gets up and grabs a towel from the bathroom. He hands me one and I clean myself up. I slip my panties back on but remain naked otherwise. Chad only puts his boxers back on and curls up next to me. He wraps his arms around me and kisses the back of my neck.

"Goodnight. Sleep good," he whispers in my ear.

I close my eyes and off to sleep, I go.

The next morning rolls around and I wake up in the same position we fell asleep in the night before. I hear the birds chirping outside my window and I feel like a million bucks. I have the man of my dreams laying next to me and the sun shining through my window.

I don't want to move. This moment is perfect, and I want to savor every minute of it. His soft hands wrapped around my waist and his knees lined up behind mine. I can feel his breathing on the top of my head. I want to turn around and see the innocence of his sleeping body, but I don't want to wake him.

I continue to lay here replaying last nights events through my mind. Dinner was amazing, our walk down the strip, with the fresh breeze blowing my hair, was wistful, and the end of the night's events couldn't have been fierier.

My mood is blissful and jubilant. I can't wait to get up and get my day started knowing I had last night to remember. There will be a skip in my step every time I think of last night.

Son. Of. A. Bitch. Rey! How could I forget about Rey? I'm an awful person. My best friend is missing and I'm sitting here gloating over my orgasm last night. I need to check my phone to see if I have any missed texts or calls. I would think Detective Marshall would be calling me anytime.

I reach for my phone as I hear Chad whimper. He doesn't want me to move. He's just as comfortable as I am. A part of me wants to put my phone down and go back to soaking up his scent but the loyal side of me says it's time to get up and get moving.

My phone says it's right at eight a.m. I'm sure Detective Marshall hasn't even read the report yet. I didn't have any missed calls. I have a text from Mark checking to see if I'm okay. I ignore it. I don't feel so guilty now, so I squirm back to my position next to Chad.

He whimpers again. It's adorable. I can't wait to see the scruffiness of his beard trembling down his neck. To be able to see his blue eyes open and me being the first thing he sees, that's an aspiration I didn't even realize I had.

Oh no, what do I look like? My mint! I slide my hand over to my nightstand and open it slowly. I try not to make any noise unwrapping my Lifesaver. I slip it into my mouth without disturbing the sexy man next to me.

How did I get here? Oh right, I threw up on him. How is this even possible? There must be something wrong with him. If he's attracted to a girl who throws up on him, he has issues. If he threw up on me, I would instantly be disgusted. But at the same time, I would look in his eyes and try to lick the remaining puke off his face.

I'm really fucked up this morning. What did he do to me? Is his cum really poison? Did he poison my soul with dumbness? He probably did. That's what's wrong with him; toxic cum. Oh, but his jawline, his facial hair, his perfectly sculpted nose and cheek bones, those sharp blue eyes, his poison is welcome. Give me all of your poison, Chad.

I feel movement behind me. There's pressure in his arm as he pulls me close to him. Now it's my turn to whimper.

He brings his mouth to my ear, "Good morning."

"Hi."

"Did you sleep okay?" he asks.

"I did. And you?"

"Like I was sleeping in a hotel."

Is that a compliment? I don't even care at this moment.

He rolls to his back and I roll over to and lay on his chest. Mental note; write a thank you letter to the man who invented the mint Lifesaver.

He's as dreamy as I imagined he would be. His beard has trickled down his neck and is as sharp as a razor blade. Oh well, cut me, Chad. His eyes are sleepy, but it doesn't keep the deep blue from peaking through. I get comfortable on his bare chest as I rub my fingers up and down his abs. Our naked bodies lie next to one another and our hearts beat in unison. Serenity overcomes me, and I close my eyes inhaling the leftover of last night's scent of cologne. He caresses my shoulder with his fingertips and we enjoy just being with one another.

He scoots down the bed and even's his eyes with mine. I wrinkle my nose at him and he smiles.

"You think you're cute, don't you?" he asks playfully.

"Maybe a little."

"I really need to get up. Have you heard anything from Detective Marshall, yet?"

"Not yet, but I figure it's still early. I'm going to try to call Rey's father again in a little while. He should be at work now, I'll try to catch him on his lunch break."

Looking in his eyes, I see paradise, I could stay here forever. Only, I can't. I have to find Rey. I have to be at work at one this afternoon; that gives me five hours to find a clue somewhere. I need to make some calls. I need to talk to Carson to see if he's heard anything.

"Do you have to work today?" I ask him. I had to work with his brother Caleb yesterday. Only, Caleb didn't do much. He sat in the chair all afternoon, again. He doesn't converse much. I bet that he gets that from his mother. The other two are pretty out-going from what I've seen.

"Yeah, it's my first day working there. What about you? Do you work today?" he asks.

"I go in at one to close."

"I don't even know what I'm supposed to do. Mom just told me to be security. To watch you girls and to make sure you guys get to your cars safe. Most importantly, according to my mother, make sure the safe is locked. Detective

Marshall and I discussed this as well. He suggested that I take notes of the customers. To note the repeaters and new customers."

"That's a pretty good idea," I say. My phone buzzes. I quickly roll over to grab my phone from the night stand. "It's Carson."

"Hello?" I say still laying in bed.

"Kat, have you heard anything?" he asks frantically.

"No, I sure haven't. I take it you haven't, either?" I say.

"No. I'm waiting to hear from the police. I did talk to Rey's father. I told him everything. He will probably call you, but he said he was going to head to the station and talk to the detectives directly. He's worried sick."

I didn't even know Carson knew her father. How come I didn't know that?

"We are all worried sick. I feel helpless," I say.

"I'm going to head to the gym and see if there's any footage of her there from Sunday." Carson is impressing me. He's going above and beyond over Rey. He's either worried the police are going to suspect him or he's just in love with her and doesn't know it.

"That's a great idea. Let me know what you find out. I have to go to work. I was going to check her room again to see if there was anything out of place."

"Ok, I'll keep you informed."

"Thanks, Carson." I hang up the phone and roll back over to Chad.

"Still nothing?" he asks.

"No, he's going to check the gym and her dad is going to the station now."

"I see. Well, I better get up. Mom opens the store at nine, I need to be there."

"You have to work ten hours? That's gross."

"Tell me about it. At least it's only three days a week." He stands up and puts his clothes on from last night. He still looks sexy in his wrinkled clothes.

"Do you want some breakfast before you head to the store? I can make you some eggs. Who knows when you'll get a lunch break." I suggest food because I'm not ready for him to leave. I want to soak up every moment I can.

I'm glad he's working with me today, but also worried it may be a little awkward. The morning after isn't too weird, but in a professional setting, around his mother especially, things could get awkward real fast.

"That would be great. Thank you." He walks to the bathroom and I scramble to get dressed. I'm okay with being naked under the covers but uncomfortable just letting it all hang out in daylight.

I pull my hair back into a low ponytail and throw on a gray sweater with black leggings. I head to the kitchen and pull out a skillet. I grab some vegetable oil and some eggs from the fridge.

I turn on a pot of coffee as I hear him coming down the hallway and he sits on a barstool. He's quiet as he's scrolling through his phone. I grab a plate from the cabinet and sit it in front of him.

"How do you like your eggs?" I ask.

"Scrambled is fine. Thank you," he says. "How do you like your eggs?" he asks.

"I'm allergic to eggs."

"Really? I've never met anyone allergic to eggs. Almost everything has egg in it. What do you eat?" he asks intrigued.

"I eat a lot of protein; chicken, turkey, peanuts."

"Can you have bread?" he asks.

"Well, I eat it and I'm not dead, so yeah," I laugh at myself.

He smiles and goes back to scrolling through his phone while I finish cooking. I grab a coffee cup from the cup hook and pour him a cup.

"Do you want milk or sugar?" I ask him.

"Milk, thanks. Wait, there's only one cup. Don't tell me you don't like coffee?"

"I like latte's but I'm not a big fan of black coffee," I say.

"You're a special breed, aren't you?" he laughs.

"I'm something, alright. You'll come to find out I'm very peculiar, as my mom says. I like what I like, I don't like what I don't like and there's no changing my mind. And if you get me laughing hard enough, I snort."

"Challenge accepted." He winks at me as he begins to eat his eggs. I grab a pre-packaged bag of donuts out of the cabinet and pour me a glass of milk. His phone is going off quite a bit for it to be so early.

"Everything okay?" I ask trying to be nonchalantly nosey.

"Yeah, I have just got to get going. Mom needs me down at the store right away."

"Oh, okay." I grab his plate and put it in the sink. "I'll see you at work then?"

"Yeah." He's hustling to put on his shoes.

"Wait, Chad." I stop him while he's unlocking the door. "Aren't you going to ask for my number?

"No." He walks out.

Chapter 10

My morning has been hectic. Making calls, receiving calls, pacing the neighborhood, I can't sit still. I walk in to work not knowing what to expect. My mind has been rushing non-stop since Chad walked out the door. He sleeps with me, but won't take my number? I couldn't even concentrate talking to Rey's father.

Detective Marshall called and said he would investigate and do the best he could. He wouldn't go into detail about his plans but assured he would start on it right away.

Carson plans on hitting the pavement and checking every dumpster around the neighborhood. The thought of it is shivering. She's not in a dumpster. She's somewhere alive. I just know it. She's smart, she'll figure something out.

I walk behind the counter and see Samantha making a coffee. I put my purse underneath the register and put my phone in my back pocket in case someone tries to call.

"Hey, you, what's going on?" she asks.

"Where's our new boss?" I ask.

"He's in one of the aisle's somewhere. Why, what's up? Everything okay?"

"Um, yeah," I say hesitantly, "just wanting to know what the new plans are here. If he's really going to boss us around or if Kathy is still our boss." I walk away still speaking.

I peak around the corner of the aisle and it's empty. I head to the next aisle and see him standing with his back to me.

"Chad?"

He turns around and I see Jane standing on the other side of him. What is she doing here?

"Oh, hey, Kat," Jane speaks while Chad stands silent.

I look at him and then look at her. She puts her hand on his bicep and says, "I'll text you later. Have a good day." She walks past me with a smile on her face, "Bye, Kat."

What the hell just happened? He obviously communicates with her on the telephone, why not me? Did I get played?

I turn my head back towards him while he stands there with his hands in his pockets. I stare him down hoping he realizes I'm pretty aggravated at this point.

What happened to the affection of him holding me? The morning conversation over breakfast? Is this his game? Does he do this with all the girls? Why does Jane get to touch his arm while I'm standing here looking at him like a deer in headlights?

I am stunned by his behavior. I have to shake this off. I have other important things to be concerned about than Jane having his number, but not wanting mine.

I turn around and walk behind the counter. I don't even have anything I want to say to him. I just want to make a vanilla latte and start stocking shelves.

"Did you find him?" Sam asks.

"Yeah, he was busy. Do you mind if I stock shelves for awhile and you take care of the register? I need to clear my head.

"You okay?" she asks.

"Yeah, just got a lot going on at the moment. Thank you."

I grab one of the boxes stacked next to the wall and head back on the floor. The store has a few customers, nothing that Samantha can't handle by herself.

I head to the back aisle to where I can have some privacy. Chad walks out of the office, I ignore him. I casually look around to see where he's going. He takes a seat in one of the wingback chairs up front. It must be rough having the job of sitting in a bookstore all day.

I start unloading the boxes and putting the books on the shelf. My mind begins to wander. I replay last nights' and this mornings' conversations through my mind, again. Did I say something to upset him? Did I talk to much and annoy him? I'm at a loss here.

Better yet, who the hell does he think he is? I don't need his number. I don't need him. I've been living the last 23 years of my life without him, I can continue. Why am I so hung up on this? Get it together, Kat.

Let's think about where Rey is. Where she could have went? Why would anyone take her if she was abducted? I have no answers to these questions. If her dad doesn't know anything, Carson doesn't know anything, and none of our friends know anything, something bad must be going on.

Chad is wrong. How am I supposed to sleep at night knowing my friend is missing? Well, you had no problem sleeping last night, did you Kat? I'm pissing myself off.

Seriously, though. In all reality, the bookstore gets robbed, almost gets robbed again, we get robbed and now my best friend is missing. Whatever the Lakes' are into, is trickling into my life and in a dangerous manner.

I start thinking about different scenarios. What is Rey's routine? She had left the play and went to the gym. The surveillance camera at the gym shows her leaving around seven p.m. I had a meeting here at the store and then Chad came over for a little bit. It was a normal day. She would probably have grabbed something to eat before coming home or going to Carson's.

I should text Carson telling him to check out restaurants surveillance recordings as well. Let's see if we can piece anything together. Carson also suggested we put something on the social media sights to get her face out there. It's a good idea, we were just waiting on what Detective Marshall had to say.

The door bell dings, customers in and out all afternoon. The store has been busy since we put a sign in the window stating we gourmet coffee.

Rain must be on the way because it's starting to cloud over the strip. Patrons are making their way out of the store to beat getting caught in the storm. This gives me an opportunity to start studying for finals.

It's going to be hard to concentrate for multiple reasons, one being Rey, the other being Captain Douchebag over there. I need to focus on what's best for me right now. Right now, there's nothing I can do about Rey. As hard as it is to accept, I have to be realistic. I could talk to Chad, but I'm not bringing my personal insecurities to work with me.

I walk to the non-fiction section of the bookstore and search for a History & Theory book to relate to my final exam. I didn't bring my books to the store, but at least I have access to some references here.

It starts to rain pretty heavy. The doorbell rings, someone must be trying to get out of the rain. I don't blame them. Come in for a hot coffee, relax and let the storm pass. It sounds like a perfect afternoon for me.

I see Chad stand up and go to the counter to talk to Sam. "I'm going to go grab some lunch really quick while the place is pretty quiet. I'll be right back. I'm just running next door. You feel okay with that?"

Sam replies, "Yeah, I think we are fine. When you get back, I'm going to go to lunch, as well."

"Do you want me to grab you something? It's raining pretty hard out there," Chad asks Sam.

"Do you mind?"

"No, not at all," Chad reassures.

"Great. Let me write it down." Sam grabs a pen and a Post-it. "Let me get you some cash.'

"No, I'm not worried about it. It's on me," Chad says as he walks out the door.

Did he just hit on Sam? It's kind of rude that he didn't even ask if I wanted anything. I walk over behind the counter.

"Did you just see that?" Samantha asks. "He just went to get us lunch. I might ask him to go for a drink some time."

My stomach is beginning to turn, and my blood starts to boil. How dare she? How dare he? I am standing right here! I'll give Sam a bit of credit, she doesn't know about anything, but for Chad not to turn around and ask if I wanted anything, that's rude. Especially after I made him breakfast.

Why do I do this to myself? I'm beating myself up over something I can't control, again. Maybe he's just being friendly so she really doesn't have to go out in the rain. Or he's just a big prick trying to make me jealous. Well, guess what dickhead, it's working. Now hurry back.

This obsession has come on quick and is becoming extreme. I know better, but yet, I'm not stopping. I can't help but wonder if he's into me or if he played me. He duped me. I can't believe I fell for it.

I need to stop this and just concentrate on Rey and finals. I open up the book behind the counter and start to read. My mind is everywhere. I can't focus. What time is it? How long has Chad been gone? How long is it going to be raining? What time is Samantha's shift over? I need to know.

"Hey, Samantha, what time do you leave today?" I ask.

"I got here at nine, so I'll leave at three-thirty. I think I *am* going to ask Chad out for drinks tonight. The more I think about it, the more I want to."

Bitch, I will trip you right into that stack of books. Okay, Katy, calm your tits. Chad is not your boyfriend, hell, Samantha isn't even a friend, she's a co-worker. I try to tell myself that I'll be fine but if I have to watch them flirt back and forth, I'll either just ask to switch my days or I'll just quit altogether.

A few moments past, and the doors' bell rings and it's the customer leaving. The rain started to die down a bit, so I guess he decided to run. Chad holds the door open for him as the customer leaves.

Chad walks over to the counter, I still go breathless when seeing him. Hopefully, that will pass soon.

He sets the sandwich bag on the counter and says, "I didn't know what to get you to drink, so I went with a Coke, I hope that's okay?"

"Yes, that's perfect. Thank you very much," Samantha replies with a smile in her eyes.

I want to punch her eye right now.

"Speaking of drinks, do you want to get a drink sometime?" she asks.

He looks down and pauses for a moment, he looks up with grim on his face, "I'm sorry, but I'm kind of seeing someone," he replies.

Wait, did he and Jane get back together? Is that why she was here? She must have known he was working today. He did play me! I guess I deserve it; I was too eager after all. Talk about a punch to the stomach. Now, more than ever, have I wanted to puke on him on purpose. But instead, I put my head down and walk back to the aisle in which I was stacking books.

Maybe this is a good thing, he was distraction, after all. I feel guilty about what Rey.

I should be doing more to help find her. I should be making flyers, talking to everyone up and down the strip, that should be me. Why am I letting Detective Marshall tell me that he's going to handle this? Why should I trust him? There has to be many other cases he's working on as well, how can he manage all of them at once? He can't. Rey needs me.

I pull out my phone and text Carson. 'Have you heard anything?'

'Not yet.'

'I get off work at 7, meet me at the apartment.'

'Okay,' Carson replies.

I put my cell phone back in my pocket and get back to work.

The bookstore is vacant. Not many people are on the strip in general. I make a vanilla latte and sit in the front of the store on a high-top table with my book to study. Samantha comes and sits across from me while Chad heads to the back office. I notice he checks the back door to make sure it's locked.

"Well, I asked him out for drinks, but he said he's seeing someone," Sam says trying to start a conversation with me.

"Yeah, I heard." I don't want to talk about him to her. I'm already upset about the thought of him and Jane back together.

"That girl is one lucky girl," she says with disappointment in her tone.

"I don't know why they have us both here on a day like today. Would it be that Chad would send you home early or would it be Kathy?" I say trying to change the subject.

"I'm not sure. I know she said whoever was on duty we are supposed to report to. I can't imagine Chad sending me home, though. He doesn't seem like the business type."

"Ah, I wouldn't be so sure. From my understanding, he and his family are both pretty intelligent," I say indirectly defending him.

"Andrea told me that he only went to Midtown, though."

"What's wrong with Midtown? That's where I go," I say intensified.

"Oh, sorry. I wasn't trying to offend you. It's just Midtown is so—"

"So, what? Local?"

"Yes."

"I don't understand why people keep saying that. I don't run into a lot of people I went to high school with."

"Hmm, well that's not the point. The point is, Chad might be nice to look at, but may not have the brains to back it up."

Now I'm really aggravated.

"I only met Chad a few weeks ago, but from what I've seen, he's quite intelligent. He has a knack for knowing what's going to happen before it happens. Notice how he left us today, when he wasn't supposed to? He wouldn't leave us if he thought we were in any danger. He's a cop for a reason."

"Yeah, I guess you're right. But, maybe he doesn't understand the business, like Kathy thinks he does," she replies.

I never asked him when he worked at the bookstore. Was it during his college years, as well? I have nothing to say in regard to her statement.

Chad comes back out of the office. He walks over behind the counter closest to our table. "Samantha, you can take off early. It's dead in here. Your girls' paycheck is on top of the safe as well."

"Oh, well, I guess that answers my question about him being in charge," I say with a little gloat in *my* tone.

Samantha and I both stand up and walk around to the back of the counter.

"Andrea, Katy, Samantha," Samantha reads aloud. "Here you go," she says handing me my check.

I rip it open to see how much money I get to spend. We get paid bi-weekly, so this is my first check since I've started. I made two hundred and forty dollars. Is that right? I checked the paystub for accuracy; everything seems to be right. I'll save the forty dollars and spend the rest on some new summer clothes. After finals, Rey and I are going to South Carolina for a few days.

Rey. I check the time, it's only three. It's going to be a long evening. Hopefully Carson hears something from Detective Marshall before the end of the day.

"Well, I'm out of here. Chad, thanks for lunch." Sam walks out the door and I put my check in my purse. Chad still hasn't said anything to me, yet. He walks back to the office and I walk back over to the table where I was sitting.

I keep checking my phone to see if Carson has messaged me, but nothing so far. The hours drag on, no one wants to come in on a day like today. I don't even want to be here.

Today is a day to be watching reality television shows, if I had a tv, I probably would be. Maybe I should buy a tv. Rey and I always said if we are home and bored enough to watch tv, then we should be out of the house doing something adventurous. I don't know how walking up and down the strip is *adventurous*, but these days, apparently it is dangerous.

I'm off work tomorrow and I don't have class. This Sunday is my Sunday to work, but for the next two days I can dedicate to finding Rey.

The door bell rings and Chad walks back up front.

"Hi," I say to the male customer who walks by me.

The male doesn't respond but continues walking to the back aisle looking in the non-fiction section. Chad walks up and down the aisles pretending to be a customer as well.

I wonder if Chad has a gut feeling. Now, I am starting to have a gut feeling. My anxiety rises higher than normal. I try to stay calm. He's just a customer, like every other customer. I should stock something to keep me busy.

I open up the snack cabinet and restock the waters in the fridge. I wipe down the coffee counter and turn on some water in the sink to wash the utensils. I notice the music is dull over the speakers, so I turn it up a little bit more trying to give this place some atmosphere.

My phone buzzes in my back pocket. I pull it out; it's a text message from Carson.

'I just hung up with Detective Marshall, coming to bookstore now.'

I wonder if that's a good thing, or a bad thing.

Before I know it, the door bell rings and it's Carson.

"You got here fast," I say impressed.

"Yes, sorry, I was in the apartment," he says.

"My apartment?"

"Yeah, Rey made me a key last week since I get off work late sometimes and want to come over."

"Well, that would have been nice to know," I say. "What's going on?"

I hear Chad's phone ring.

Carson looks around to see if anyone is listening. "Detective Marshall called and said they might have a lead. There's a video showing her on the strip with a man holding her arm walking her around the corner of gym," he says in a high-speed voice.

"Do they know who it was?" I ask.

"No. But they are going to continue watching the videos from other businesses outside cameras to see if they see the man again. They are going now to gather the videos. They will have the night shift crew watch them tonight and will get back to me in the morning."

Chad comes walking up and uses a low tone of voice, "Carson, I just got off the phone with Detective Marshall. That's good news. When this guy leaves I'm going to replay our surveillance and see if there's anything on there. We already have a general idea but maybe our cameras can pick up a face to match the profile."

"What can I do?" I ask.

"You can continue working," Chad says sternly.

I hear the rain beat against the window. The storm is only getting stronger. The customer walks up to the counter and hands me the book he's purchasing.

"How are we doing?" Chad says to the man.

The man doesn't respond only nods his head towards him.

"It's thirteen twenty-two," I say.

The man takes off his gloves and unfolds his wallet. He gives me two fives and four ones. He grabs his book and starts to walk off.

"Sir, your change?" I say trying to stop him.

"Keep it, Katy."

And he's gone.

Chapter 11

"What the fuck was that?" I say scared.

"That was him," Chad says.

He runs to the door and looks out; both sides of the street are empty. Chad runs down the strip around the corner. Carson picks up the phone and calls Detective Marshall.

"Yes, Detective Marshall, Carson Wilson. We are at the Pond's Paperbacks and we are pretty sure the guy was just in here. Chad is outside trying to chase him down now. He knows who Katy is."

Chad comes back in the store sopping wet. "He's gone."

"Chad is back, he's gone," he says. "Ok, we'll see you soon." Carson hangs up the phone.

"Katy, did you know that man?" Chad asks me.

"No! How did he know me!" I yell.

"Wait, give me that money he just gave you," Chad says.

I'm at a stand-still. I didn't even realize I was paralyzed by this. I open the register and go to reach for the money.

"Wait, I'll do it," Chad says as he walks around the counter. He grabs a paperclip and carefully slides it onto the bills.

"What are you doing?" I ask.

"Fingerprints. It might take a while to receive the results, but if he's in the system, we will find him."

"That's a good idea," Carson says. "Katy, you need to try to calm down. Do you want me to call Mark? You probably shouldn't stay at home tonight."

At home. No, of course not. I'm not going back there. Not without an army of people with me, there's no chance in hell I'm stepping foot in that apartment.

I turn and look at Chad, his face is stone. "Yes, please call him. Tell him to get here right away."

"Let's just wait and see what the Detective has to say before we go making plans," Chad suggests.

Carson walks off to use the phone. Chad goes back to carefully trying to paperclip the dollar bills. I try to breathe.

How could this person know my name? Has he been watching me? If so, how long? Why would he want Rey and now me? Was Rey into something I didn't know about? She has been absent a lot lately.

Carson comes walking back up, "Mark is on his way."

"Thank you. I need to call my mom. Chad, can I step away for a minute?"

"No. I need you right here," he demands. "You know what you can do? You can call my mother. She needs to be here. Tell her to bring my father."

"I don't even know your fathers name?"

"Charles."

I pick up the phone and call Kathy. "Kathy, It's Katy."

"What's wrong dear?" she asks. She must be able to hear the shake in my voice.

"He was here."

"Who was here? Honey, where's Chad?"

"The thief was here! He knew my name! The cops are on their way!"

"Katy, breathe, sweetheart. Let me talk to Chad."

"He told me to call you, he's busy with fingerprints. He told me to have you bring Charles with you."

"He wants his father there? We're on our way."

She hangs up on me. What's that about? That doesn't even matter.

Chad continues to work on his fingerprints and Carson is pacing the floor. The rain is still hammering on the windows and the thunder is getting louder. I see red and blue lights pull up. Detective Marshall comes walking in with Officer Shepard.

"Officer Lakes, what are you doing?" Detective Marshall asks.

"Fingerprints. He took his gloves off to pay cash," Chad replies.

"Not a bad idea. I've taught you well," he winks at Chad. "But, Chad, let Luke take over now. I'm going to need a statement from you. Why don't we take a seat over here," Detective Marshall points to the chairs in the middle of the store.

Carson, Chad and I walk over and sit down in the chairs arranged in a circle. Carson notices I'm still shaking. He puts his hand on my shoulder for comfort.

"Just breathe. We're going to find this guy," he says trying to calm me.

"Ok, Katy, I know this must have been scary for you, so why don't we make ourselves more comfortable. Do you want a water or anything?"

"No, Detective, I'm fine. Thanks."

"Well, first off, call me Jim. It seems we are going to be spending some time together, you should feel comfortable with me," he says.

"Okay."

"Now tell me what happened."

"Well, nothing serious. Just a normal customer coming into the store. He went to the back aisle and started looking at books. About ten minutes later, or so, he comes to the counter. He took his gloves off—"

"He was wearing gloves? What kind of gloves?" Jim asks.

"Just everyday normal black Isotoner gloves. I didn't think anything of it, customers come in all the time wearing gloves. This is Connecticut."

"Okay, what book did he buy?"

"Murder in the Heartland," I say.

"That didn't seem striking to you?"

"Well, no. Not at first. Not until just now, actually. People buy murder books all the time—Oh my gosh, Rey!" I stand up in a panic.

"Kat, you need to stay calm," Chad says as he tries to grab my hand.

I jerk my hand away, "Don't you tell me to stay calm! My best friend is missing and the person who has her is buying murder books!"

"Katy, he's right. I need you to remain calm." Jim says.

Chad interrupts, "You! This is my family here! This guy has been after us for a month now. It's not just about you, Katy!" Chad yells at me.

"Guys, whatever animosity you have between the two of you, needs to stop right now. We have a job to do here and we can't do it with the two of you bickering. Do you we have an understanding?

"Yes, sorry," I say.

"We have to get a description of this guy," Jim says. "Katy, can you remember anything about him?"

"I don't know, I can't think straight, right now. We have cameras, watch them," I demand. I'm aggravated with the questions. "I can't do this right now. He knows my name. How does he know my name? Am I next?"

I can see the fear in Carson's eyes. "Look at him. He is a grown man and he is scared; how do you expect me not to be?" I say.

The men look at Carson as he is sitting up with his elbows on his knees and hands covering the top of his eyes. He's tapping his foot on the ground trying to release the built-up energy boiled up inside.

"He's a nervous wreck. All three of us were standing right next to him and not a one of us noticed. He knew what he was doing! We didn't have a clue! Well, not until he called me by my name!"

I start pacing back and forth behind the chairs the men are sitting in before Jim stops me. "Katy, please. I know this is hard for you, but I can't move forward until we get a statement."

I walk back over to my chair and sit down. "Okay, what's next?"

Jim asks, "Have you ever seen this man before?"

"No, never. But I've only been working here for a few short weeks. I can't figure out why this person would want Rey?"

"No one ever said this is the person related to Rey. We have no idea if this man knows anything about Rey. There is nothing showing that the robbery here and your friend are related," Jim makes a point.

"So, what then? This could just be the thief fucking with us?" I ask.

"Unfortunately, yes," Jim confirms. "Did he say anything to you, Carson?"

Carson looks up, suddenly he calms, "No, actually he didn't."

"Chad, did he say anything to you?" Jim asks.

"No. I asked how he was doing, just normal greeting, and he just nodded to me. It wasn't anything out of the ordinary a man would do."

My nerves calm a bit. "So, what if this isn't related to Rey? This guy still knows my name. He's obviously been watching me. Could this be the same guy who broke into our apartment?" I say looking at Chad.

"Possibly. Look, there are many options here. We have to take it one step at a time."

"Well, you take it one step at a time. My steps are locking myself into a hotel room where no one can get to me," I say.

"That's actually a pretty good plan, Katy," Detective Marshall agrees. "This way, we know you're locked in, we can monitor the hotel closely, we can watch for any unusual behavior. I'm not saying this is related to you directly, but we need to take proper precautions."

"Alright, well let's go," I say wanting to get the hell out of here.

"Not so fast," Chad says. "We still have things to do here."

"You're serious right now? You want me to stay here working for you? What the hell is wrong with you?"

"Katy—"

"Chad, she's right. She's in no condition to stay here," Jim says.

"Fine, then I'm going with you," Chad says.

"The hell if you are!" I say. "You have work to do!"

"Kat!" Carson yells. "You've got to breathe. Mark will be here any second, okay?"

"Who's Mark?" Detective asks.

"Katy's boyfriend," Carson says.

"Boyfriend?" both Chad and Jim say in unison.

"No, he's not my boyfriend. He's just a friend. Really, Carson? It's not the time to be making jokes," I snap at him.

"I'm not making jokes. Mark is your best option right now. He can stay at the hotel with you so you're not alone. You trust him enough to know he's not going to let anything happen to you. Quit being so damn stubborn and listen to one of us," Carson snaps back. "I'm not playing the invisible game today. You're going to listen to me or you're going to wind up missing, like Rey."

That hit me hard. I've never seen this side of Carson before. No wonder Rey is attracted to him. He has a backbone.

The next thing I know Kathy and Charles are walking through the back. Charles is tall like Chad. He's got a husky build and a clean-shaven face. He is who the boys get their eyes from. His father must have been one to tame back in the day.

"Chad!" Katy exclaims. "My goodness, are you okay?"

Chad stands up and walks over to his parents. "Mother, I'm fine," he says. "Dad."

"Hi, son."

"Guys, this is Detective Marshall, with the Middletown Police Department," Chad introduces them.

I see Marks face. I block out everything going on around me. I need him. I stand up and walk swiftly to him.

"Kat, what's going on? Are you hurt?"

I don't answer I just wrap myself up in his arms. He takes his hand to the back of my head and holds me close.

"Hey now, you're okay," he says.

I can feel the tears coming on now that the adrenaline is dying down. I bite my tongue to keep from crying. I need to get out of here.

I walk over to Kathy, "Kathy, is it okay if I go ahead and leave for the day?"

Kathy pulls me into her arms, "Oh, I'm so glad you're okay." She puts her hands on me arms and pulls me back within arms-length and looks me in the eyes and pulls me back into her arms. "I really am glad you're okay."

I stand up straight, "Thanks. But do you mind if I take off? I need to pack a bag and get some place safe."

"I don't mind, but Chad is your boss. You'll need to ask him," she says looking in his direction.

I turn to look at him with malevolent eyes, "Can I?"

"No."

"Chad!" I yell.

"Son, let her go home. She's obviously in distress," Charles says.

Chad gives his father the same look I just gave to him. "Fine. But I'm closing this place up, then."

"That's fine, son. You're obviously in distress as well," Kathy says.

"Thank you," I say to Kathy.

"Get some rest, sweetheart," she replies.

I turn around to Detective Marshall, "Are we done here?"

"For now. But, I need to know where you're going tonight," We will set up a team at the hotel and put even more patrol on the store. I'll have a cop car outside these doors all night," he says looking back and forth between me and the Lakes' family.

"I will call you when I find out where I'm staying. Can I ask that Officer Shepard does a walk-thru of my apartment before I go in?" I ask.

"Yes, of course," Jim says. "Luke," his head pops up, "can you escort Miss Cambridge home and then to wherever she is staying?"

"Absolutely." Luke walks around the counter and waits for me by the door.

Carson stands up to follow while Mark heads towards the door. I have quite of a security team with me, right now.

It's still raining heavily, I would prefer if Luke would go ahead and do his walk-thru before I leave the store. I walk behind the counter to get my keys.

"Officer Shepard, would you mind checking out the apartment first before I leave here?"

"I'll go with him," Mark says. "Do you want me to pack you a bag, so you don't have to go upstairs?"

"That would be great. Just something to sleep in, and a couple outfits. There's jeans in the bottom drawer of my dresser. Any top will be fine," I say to him with sincerity. "Thank you, Mark."

"I'll head upstairs with them," Carson says.

I throw my keys to Carson and they hustle to the street door. I put my paycheck in my purse and clock out on the register. The Lakes' converse with Detective Marshall while I gather my thoughts.

Chad leaves their conversation and walks over to me. "Do you know where you're going to stay yet?"

"No. I'm thinking about that now. I'm thinking I should go downtown to get away from this area."

"I think that's a smart idea. Make sure Luke takes you and escorts you inside. Don't let him leave your side. Jim is setting up extra security for you around the hotel and Mom is going to call Caleb to have security set up for you outside your door."

"Outside my door? Don't you think that's a little much?"

"Dad suggested it. We do what Dad says," he replies.

"Okay, well if you guys insist."

"Katy, it's not time to be catty. That sounded funny," he laughs trying to lighten the mood.

There it is; my heart skipping a beat. His smile is humbling and puts me at ease.

"Just do what they say. You're off the next couple of days, try to get some rest. I would stay at the hotel as long as you can. Mom wants to pay for it, you should let her."

"That's not necessary," I say. Then, I remember my paycheck and how I can't afford to stay at the hotel for long. "Does she have a suggestion on where I should stay?"

"We have connections at the Inn on Main. It's basically a Marriot. It should have everything you could need in case the guys forget something."

"Alright." I pull out my phone to Google the number to make a reservation. I hit the call button and Chad jerks it out of my hand. "What the hell?"

"I told you, Mom has connections there. Let us set it up for you," he says.

"Okay, fine. Set it up for me."

"When the guys get back down here, I'll tell Luke to take you straight there. Don't leave for food, or anything. The hotel has room service. Don't even go out in the hall," he demands.

I jerk my phone out of his hand, "Thanks."

Chad turns his back to me, "Hey, Mom, she agreed to stay at the Inn, will you call and get it set up, please?"

"I'll do it. She needs to call your brother," Charles says.

Detective Marshall walks towards us, "Alright, I have everything I need from you guys. Chad is going to email me the surveillance videos and we'll get started right away. I've called the station, they are having a car meet you at the hotel until," looking at Chad, "your brother's team gets there."

"Thank you for everything, Jim," I say.

"You're welcome. Try to get some rest. You'll be safe there." He opens the door with pounding rain still beating down onto the sidewalks.

"It's nasty out there. I hope the guys hurry back soon," I say walking back to the wing-back chair I was sitting in.

"They'll be back anytime, now," Chad says.

Kathy and Charles walk over towards us. I do wonder how Kathy suppressed his raw sexuality. He must have had women tripping over him. I wonder if he's been faithful during their forty years of marriage; I bet not.

"Katy, is it?" Charles confirms.

"Yes, sir," I respond.

"Call me 'Charles,'" he says. I nod my head. "I've got you set up at the Inn. Caleb and his team are headed there now. Officer Shepard will take you there. I do suggest that no one accompanies you tonight. Our security teams need to focus on you, and you only. Do you understand?"

"Yes, yes of course."

"Chad, you need to close up shop and get somewhere safe, as well. If this is directed at our family, we need to take proper precautions for everyone. Caleb is sending someone to drive you, as well."

"Bullshit. I'm a grown man. I can handle myself," he replies.

"Son, this is not up for negotiation. You will do what I say," Charles states.

Well, we know who the boss is in the Lakes' house. I bet he put the fear of God into the boys when they were younger. No wonder they've all grown up to be successful individuals; they grew up in a home of discipline.

It also brings Chad's decision to be a cop, to a full circle. When he was old enough to make his own decisions, he defied their wishes. It makes sense that might be why Kathy resents Midtown so much.

"I'll be fine at my place, it has security at the door. No one is going to mess with me," Chad argues.

"I said this wasn't a negotiation, you won't leave here until Caleb's driver gets here. Do we have an understanding?"

Chad's stern face falls flat; it's a face of defeat. "Yes, sir."

The door chimes, "Miss Cambridge, the apartment is clear. I have your bag and I am ready when you are," Luke says. Mark and Carson follow him in to get out of the rain.

"Are you ready to go?" Mark asks.

I walk closer to him. "Actually, I'm going to stay alone tonight. It's best for everyone's safety. There's no reason for you to put yourself in the line of danger."

"No, I'm not leaving you," Mark argues.

"Yes, really. I am going to be fine. I'll let you know when I get to the hotel." I don't have him a chance to respond and walk out the door.

I get in the car, trying to gather my composure. I look through the bag Luke grabbed for me. I have something to sleep in and some jeans and a sweater for tomorrow. They forgot my toothbrush but did remember my phone charger. Hopefully the hotel has commodities.

I pick up the phone to call my mom; she's going to be so distraught. She answers after two rings.

"Hey, Sis. What's going on?"

"Hi, Mom. I just wanted to let you know I'm going to be staying at the Inn on Main downtown tonight."

"Oh, why? Does your new boyfriend live close to there?"

"No, Mom. And he's not my boyfriend. Don't freak out, but something happened at the bookstore today and my boss is paying for me to stay in a hotel for a couple days until things get cleared up."

"What? What happened? Does this have anything to do with Rey?" she asks.

"We're not sure. A suspicious man came in the store and he knew my name. Kathy doesn't know if its related to Rey or if its related to the theft recently at the store. Or both."

"Oh, Kat."

"Mom, I'm fine. We are just taking the extra precautions to be sure. I'll text you the details when I get there."

"Ok, Sis. I love you."

"Love you, too, Mom." I hang up the phone and try to soak up the peaceful atmosphere in this vehicle. I know I'm safe. I know I'm going to some place safe. I know I will have people around me who will keep me safe. There's a sense of calmness overtaking my soul at the moment.

We pull up to the Inn Hotel. There's people outside staring as we pull up in the police car. I try to ignore the stares of those surrounding the entryway.

"Okay, you wait here. I'm going inside to see if your security has arrived. Do not open these car doors for anyone except me, understand?" Luke says.

"Yes," I reply. "Please hurry."

A few moments pass, and I see Officer Shepard walking out to the vehicle followed by two men in khaki pants and matching pullovers. Both men are wearing baseball hats and tennis shoes. I can only assume Caleb wants his crew in every day attire to blend in with their surroundings. Luke taps on the window and I roll it down.

"Katy, these are the two men from Caleb's crew. This is Jake," Luke says in regard to the man on the right. Gesturing with his hand to the left, "and this is Shane." Both men appear to be in their thirties. Jake has a wedding band on, while the only jewelry Shane is wearing is a gold necklace.

"Hi," I say to both men.

Luke gestures for me to unlock the car door. I exit the vehicle with my bag and walk towards the entry door.

"Miss Cambridge, if you need anything," he hands me piece of paper, "here is my phone number. Call me day or night. Even if you just want pizza, I will bring it to you. I am on shift until seven tomorrow morning. I can be here ASAP."

"Thank you, Luke." I smile and put the number in my bag. I walk in the hotel with the two men behind me.

"You have already been checked in, Miss Cambridge," Jake says.

"Please, call me Kat. If we are going to be spending a lot of time together, we might as well be comfortable," a line I stole from Detective Marshall.

The two men guide me to the elevator door and press the number eight; the top floor. The elevator requires a key card to access the eighth floor. Shane pulls out the key card from his pocket and slide it into the elevator slot.

"There's only four suites on the eighth floor and two of them have been reserved for you and us," Shane says. "We shouldn't have much company."

"Oh, you are staying on the floor? I didn't realize—"

"Yes, we will take shifts keeping surveillance on the hotel, we will only be an adjoining door away," Jake says.

"Okay, well that makes me feel better, I say.

The elevator dings and we arrive on the eighth floor. Shane steps out in front of me and I follow him to the end of the hall.

"Our room is here," pointing to the door on the left and your room is just a few feet away, here. The staircase is at the end of the hall next to the elevator, but don't worry, it can only be accessed by one of the four room keys, as well."

Jake opens the door for me with the key. "I was advised not to give you a key, if you leave, one of us will go with you and let you back in."

I frown. Just how serious is this situation? If this is related to only the Lakes' and their robberies, what are they into to require so much security?

I walk into the hotel room. There's two rooms, one with a sofa and desk, and then the bedroom with a king size bed, a chair, and a bathroom attached. The adjoining door is immediately to my left walking in.

"We will keep these adjoining doors open. If you want privacy, your bedroom has a door on it. But we must be able to get to you immediately," Jake says.

"Okay," I say sitting my bag on the computer desk.

"Is there anything you need, are you hungry?" Shane asks.

"Actually, I am. Can we just order a pizza? I don't feel like being alone at the moment, can we just all sit here and watch a movie?" I ask.

I guess Shane finds this abnormal, "Miss Cambridge, we really aren't supposed to socialize with our clients.

"Well, that's just too bad. I'm going to take a shower and one of you order a pizza," I command. Without giving them time to respond, I shut my bedroom door and begin to undress.

I turn on the hot water and let the room begin to steam. I open up my makeup bag and luckily there is a razor still left in there from when I needed one for the play.

I jump in the shower and let the beads of water beat upon my skin. I exhale and relieve any tension I have built up inside. I reach for the shampoo and massage my own head. I wonder if there's a spa in this five-star hotel they are keeping me hostage in?

I finish washing and drying off. I start to blow dry my hair and my mind begins to wander.

"Happy Birthday Katy and Audrey, Happy Birthday to you!" Mom sings. *"Now, make a wish!"*

Both Rey and I blow out our candles. We are turning nine together. It's neat that her birthday is only a few days before mine. Once I told Mommy about Audrey having a birthday party, Mommy thought it would be fun if I had one, too. She's letting me have Audrey spend the night and we get to watch movies together.

Audrey got me a cat headband. It's black and has cat ears on it. Mommy says we just need to paint my nose black and I will be the cutest kitten on the block.

I got Audrey a new pair of earring with the letter A on them. She can wear them all the time. They will match anything my mom says.

This is the best birthday, ever. Mommy goes to get a knife out of the drawer to cut the cake and closes the drawer pretty hard. Thump.

I hear a knocking on my bedroom door.

Chapter 12

"Yeah?" I yell.

"Pizza is here!" Shane yells back.

Damn that was fast. I finish drying my hair and put it back into a low messy-bun. I put on my oversized gray Midtown hoodie and a pair of gray sweatpants and head into the sofa room.

"The hotel has a restaurant downstairs, so we just ordered a pizza from there. Hope that's okay," Jake says.

"That's perfect."

"There's drinks in the fridge and we had the staff bring up plates and napkins."

"You guys are awesome; can I keep you around always?" I ask playfully.

We kick back onto the sofa and begin to pig out. Having the opportunity to sit down and watch tv gives me a sense of tranquility.

We laugh and get to know each other on a more personal level. Jake has a wife with a baby on the way, while Shane just broke up with his girlfriend and not looking to date anyone for a while.

Suddenly, there's a knock on the door.

"What else did you guys order?" I ask.

"Nothing. It must be house-keeping," Jake says. Jake gets up and walks to the door, looking through the peep-hole, "It's Chad."

"Chad?" I ask confirming.

Jake opens the door, "What's up, Chad?"

"I need to talk to Katy. Can we have minute alone?"

The two men walk into their room while Chad goes to shut the adjoining door.

"You really aren't supposed to do that," Shane tries to halt him.

Chad goes to pull the door anyways, "Go ahead call Caleb. We'll be fine." He shuts the door and turns to face me.

"What are you doing here? Aren't you supposed to be some place safe, too?"

"I am. I'm staying the suite across the hall."

"Of course, you are," I roll my eyes while taking a bite of pizza. "Want some?" I ask with a mouthful.

"No," he replies.

"Okay? Then what are you doing here, Chad?" I ask as he's walking closer to me.

"I don't know what I'm doing," he says.

"You have some nerve showing up after the way you treated me today."

"Treated you? How about the way you treated me?" he says firing back.

"Me? You are the one who used me last night, blew me off today and then had the audacity to tell me I couldn't leave after I just went through a traumatizing occurrence. How dare you show up here trying to say I was the one in the wrong!" I yell.

"I have some nerve?" he replies. "How about you? You bring your boyfriend in and ask him to stay with you right in front of me! You want to talk about what's wrong and what's right, why don't you think before you speak," he yells back.

"Mark is not my boyfriend, how many times do I have to say that? And what about you? I get to work today, and Jane is all over you. So, don't you dare come at me about a 'boyfriend.' And to not let me call my mom? How heartless are you?"

"You're right, I'm heartless. So heartless that you think I'm just okay with you walking away by yourself? Why do you think I wouldn't let you step away to call your mom? That's because I couldn't breathe! The thought of something happening to you makes me physically ill. I thought, for once, I was going to throw up on *you*."

That makes me giggle a little, but I don't let him see.

He continues, "As for Mark staying with you tonight? I had to have my father tell you that you had to stay alone because I couldn't stand the thought of him being here alone with you! I sure as hell don't want you staying alone, but I would rather you stay alone than with him!"

I'm left speechless. I want to chew up my food, but my mouth is wide open from what he just said to me. I'm not backing down.

"You can sit here and say all of this, and try to make me forgive you, but that doesn't change the fact that you slept with me and then refused to give me your number! Then to top it off, I see Jane touching you, I see you buying Samantha lunch, all while giving me the cold shoulder! What you did to me today was purely out of spite. It was childish and self-indulgent. Now here you are trying to make up for it? Just leave!"

"You think this is coincidence? You think me staying across the hall is purely by chance? You're not a dumb girl, but right now, you're acting like it."

"A dumb girl? Get out! Leave right now!" I demand.

"No." He bails towards me and grabs my face.

Without having a chance to pull myself away, he pulls me in. I succumb to his lips as they are filled with passion and desire.

He sweeps the pizza off of the desk and sits me upon it. He takes my sweater over my head and throws it on the floor. I pull hit shirt over his head and toss it towards mine. I unbuckle his belt as he pulls my sweatpants down.

He grabs my breast with one hand while his other is holding my face against his. The anger between us only stimulates one another. His lips trickle down to my neck as goosebumps appear on my arms. He slides down to my breasts and exposes my nipples from my bra. His tongue flicks me as his hand drops down to my clit. He rubs up and down arousing my pussy. He takes two fingers and slides them inside of me. His head trickles down between my legs as his tongue takes over his hands work. He puts my legs over his shoulders and my back arches.

As my body intensity rises, I start to moan. I take my hand to the back of his head guiding him to my pleasure points. My body begins to ache for him. I put my hands on his shoulders and bring him eye-level to me.

He pulls down his pants and exposes himself. He brings my pelvis to the edge of the table and shoves his dick inside of me. He puts one hand on the small of my back bringing him deeper into me, and one hand pressed up against the wall for pressure.

Both of my arms are wrapped around his neck while he licks my chest and neck. The intensity builds as he begins to thrust harder. The momentum brings wetness to my pussy and he glides effortlessly. The deeper he goes, the more aroused I become.

I begin to moan louder as he pumps harder. The moans coming from his mouth is turning me on even more. I can't take it anymore. The walls of my vagina begin to quench around his dick. I flex my kegel muscles in conjunction with his thrusts. He takes me to the edge, and one step more. I explode around him as he erupts into me.

The heavy breathing begins to lessen as I sit here numb. He puts his pressure into his hands that are now sitting on both sides of my hips.

He doesn't say anything as he walks into the bathroom and grabs a towel. I clean myself up and get redressed.

I break the ice, "I need to go downstairs and get a toothbrush. The guys' have my keycard, can I just have yours really quick?"

"Um, no," he responds. "Did you not just listen to anything I just said? You aren't going anywhere alone. I'll go downstairs with you."

"That's fine. But, I want to go now. My teeth feel gross," I say.

We don't tell Security we are going downstairs and we are quiet closing the door.

"I'll race you," I say. Without giving him a chance to respond, I start to run towards the elevator. He tries to catch up and we hit the elevator doors at the same time. We laugh as the doors begin to close.

We walk out into the lobby where there's quite a crowd of people for the dinner rush. There's a line at the front desk so we stand in the back of the line. I see a group of chairs surrounding an indoor fireplace. There are four tall-back chairs that swivel so you can see out onto the back patio.

"I'm going to have a seat over here by the fireplace," I tell Chad.

"Alright, don't travel off. I mean it," he says.

"I won't, I'll behave," saying with a wink.

I walk over and sit in a swivel chair closest to the fireplace. There must be an event downtown this weekend as the crowd starts to pour in the hotel on a Thursday night. People maneuver around one another with their luggage trying to find access to their rooms. There are others sitting at the lobby bar enjoying their friends and significant other's conversations.

I'm enjoying watching at Chad stand in line. He nods his head to those males around him and smiles at the children walking by. The police officer persona in him is beginning to appear. I notice his gun on his hip, I never noticed it earlier.

I swivel back around to look out onto the patio when the chair in front of me swivels back to face me.

It's Rey. She looks exhausted. Her hair is a mess and has dark circles under her eyes. Her clothes look worn and her tennis shoes are dirty. Her fingernails have dirt under them as she's grasping onto my stuffed Kitty Katy.

"Oh my God, Rey!" I get up and run to her. I bow down onto my knees in front of her and grab her hands. "Oh, sweetie, are you okay?" She nods her head yes. "Rey, speak to me. Who's with you?" I look around me searching for anyone who remotely looking suspicious. I turn back around to face her, she's shaking her head.

"What, what is it?" I say frantically "Rey, talk to m—" I'm being pulled up by the back of shirt.

"Don't say a word," I hear in a husky voice whisper in my ear from behind me. "Stay calm and don't make a scene. You're going to do exactly what I say, do you understand?"

I nod my head up and down.

"You, get up," he says to Rey. She stands up and drops Kitty Katy to the floor. "Go open those doors. Don't make a sound." He pushes me out the doors to around the building. It's still raining so there's no one out here around us.

He releases my arm and throws me into Rey and we hit the brick wall. "Don't turn around, you stay right there."

The rain is pouring down on Rey and I. The raindrops are stinging my arms as they hit. "What do you want," I ask.

"Shut up! I'm the one doing the talking! Now you girls are going to listen to me very carefully. The gate is straight ahead. You walk out the gate and the car is straight ahead. Neither of you look back."

I grab Reys' wrist, searching for her fingers and we walk hand in hand to the gate while he follows closely behind. The thunder is loud and terrifying.

"Freeze, motherfucker!" I hear Chad yell.

I'm instantly flipped around and suddenly there is a gun to my neck. My eyes widen speaking to Chad begging for help.

"You stay right there, you come any closer and these girls get a bullet through their necks!" the husky voice yells.

I hear Rey humming loudly. I look to her and her mouth is glued shut. How could he do this to her? Who is this man and what does he want with us?

"You let her go, now!" Chad yells while taking a step forward.

"Put the gun down!" the husky voice yells to Chad.

"Let her go and I'll put it down."

"Chad! Just put the gun down!" I yell.

"Shut up!" the husky voices yells in my ear.

"Let her go!" Chad continues to yell.

"I don't have to let her go!" he yells. "I'm her father."

Made in the USA
Middletown, DE
27 April 2018